Readers Love GREYSON McCOY

Bridging Hope

"I truly enjoyed this short, poignant story of overcoming what life has thrown at you and rising above to succeed and live."

—Love Bytes Reviews

"Pierce and Dalton experiment, take risks, and learn that when you have kids, love alone isn't enough – the kids are the most important thing."

—Rainbow Book Reviews

Bridging Lives

"This was a sweet, gentle story…the book was easy to read and I liked the quiet feelings of coming home it gave me."

—OMG Reads

"This was a wonderful story, a story of overcoming and starting over."

—Paranormal Romance Guild

By GREYSON MCCOY

BRIDGING HEARTS
Bridging Hope
Bridging Lives
Mending Bridges

Published by DREAMSPINNER PRESS
www.dreamspinnerpress.com

Mending Bridges

GREYSON McCOY

Published by
DREAMSPINNER PRESS

8219 Woodville Hwy #1245
Woodville, FL 32362 USA
www.dreamspinnerpress.com

This is a work of fiction. Names, characters, places, and incidents either are the product of author imagination or are used fictitiously, and any resemblance to actual persons, living or dead, business establishments, events, or locales is entirely coincidental.

Mending Bridges
© 2025 Greyson McCoy

Cover Art
© 2024 Reece Notley
reece@vitaenoir.com
Cover content is for illustrative purposes only and any person depicted on the cover is a model.

Trade Paperback ISBN: 978-1-64108-794-0
Digital ISBN: 978-1-64108-793-3
Trade Paperback published January 2025
v. 1.0

With special thanks to Jo Bird and Renee Mizar.

Xander Petterson

MY HEART raced as I stepped onto the porch of the little bungalow that sat haphazardly next to one of the covered bridges on the river that divided the town of Wilcox—on one side the old part of town, and on the other, more modern homes.

I had come to call on one of the town matriarchs—Ms. Healy—to turn over a journal that had belonged to my late aunt. Unfortunately, that journal contained some very sad personal information about Ms. Healy, and since Ms. Healy had saved my friend Levi and me when we painted a couple of the nearby covered bridges without permission from the county, I felt obliged to share the journal with her.

God help me, I wished I were anywhere but there.

I hadn't even knocked before the elderly woman opened the door, her expression hard to read apart from weariness.

"Come on in. I've made you a cup of coffee. Your mother said you like it dark and bitter, with a dash of cream, so that's what I've fixed."

She pointed to the stuffy furniture to indicate where she wanted me to sit, then went to the kitchen and returned a moment later with a huge steaming mug. I'd already had too much coffee, but I understood the ritual.

"Would you like me to leave this with you?" I asked.

She stared at it for a long time. "I loved her, you know. I've never loved a woman—or man, for that matter—like I loved her." She took a deep breath and let it out slowly. "She wanted to move to Portland or Seattle. Had convinced herself we'd be more accepted there. I just couldn't see it. The world didn't allow people like us to love one another back then. But my nephew had just left for college, and she was convinced that was our time."

She glanced up at me and stubbornly wiped away an errant tear. "I should've gone. I knew it the night she left. I should've said yes. Damn it, Xander, I was afraid. Not one day of my life has passed that I haven't regretted that."

She paused a long time and then finally made eye contact. "Cid Stewart—Stewie—has been a good friend. I don't guess I have to tell you that if he finds out that the reason I've never been willing to be with him is because I'm a lesbian, that'd hurt him really bad."

I knew she was asking for discretion. Her relationships were her business, and it wasn't my place, or anyone's, to expose her sexuality or the love she had for my aunt.

I stood up. "I won't pretend this won't be hard to read. But I think, somehow, she wanted you to know how she felt. How much she loved you."

Ms. Healy gasped, and I could tell the emotions were getting the better of her, so I handed the journal to her and left her sitting alone with it and the consequences of the life she'd been forced, or felt she was forced, to choose.

I didn't expect to get the journal back. How could someone who'd loved another, only to lose them, ever give back their words when they were all they had left?

I drove back to my mom's house and sat next to her on the swing. "How'd it go?" she asked.

"As well as you'd expect," I said. She didn't respond. The journal had been heart-wrenching to read. So much had been tossed away.

"You know, back when they were young," Mom finally said, "when they were dealing with this, the world was a hateful place for women who loved one another like they did."

I did know, at least as much as someone could know when they hadn't grown up in that hateful time. "You know I told Aunt Greta I was gay before I told anyone else," I admitted.

Mom stopped her swinging and looked at me. "Really? She was in the home by then."

I nodded. "Yep, she was already in hospice, but my heart was so overwhelmed, and you know she was always someone I could talk to. Of course, I had no idea she was gay or bi herself."

Mom sighed and kicked her foot, setting the swing back into motion. "I guess that's appropriate, then. It's just so overwhelming to learn that after having grown up with her. Hell, the woman was instrumental in raising me, not to mention the fact that, even now, I consider Helen Healy a friend."

"Had things been more like they are today, she might've been your aunt."

Mom nodded, and we sat like that for a long time before she finally got up to go inside. She kissed me goodbye, since I still planned to drive up to Portland.

I stayed out on the swing thinking, even though the nights were cold and the evening chill was beginning to set in. The world had changed so much over the years.

One day I hoped to find a man I could love enough to marry. Of course, all the mushy, lovey-dovey stuff going on between Cliff and my bestie, Brandon.

But even before they found love, I think I always wanted it. I was determined to avoid the kind of relationship Aunt Greta had with her horrible husband, and Mom and Dad's relationship wasn't that stellar either. Even after Dad passed away, Mom hadn't dated anyone, at least not to my knowledge. Of course, she never talked to me about her personal life.

Regardless of my not-so-great role models, I still held out hope that I'd beat the odds where love was concerned.

But not right away. I loved men and enjoyed tasting the different fruits of the proverbial tree before I settled for just one.

I laughed at my stupid analogy, leaned back in the swing, picked my feet up, and let it go higher like I used to do as a kid.

I finally got up and headed toward my truck. I had a late-morning meeting, but more important, with all the talk of love, I craved something less permanent or heavy than all the stuff around Ms. Healy and Aunt Greta—at least for tonight.

Maybe love was in the cards, maybe not, but I'd be damned if I'd end up like my aunt and spend my life pining away for someone who didn't have the nerve to take the plunge. I liked old Ms. Healy, always had, but I couldn't help but feel resentment for how she'd left my poor aunt alone and brokenhearted.

No, I'd never end up like that, not when there were so many willing men on Grindr.

Rhys Healy

"RHYS," MY dad said through the walkie-talkie. "Come up to the office."

"Can't right now, Dad. Got to finish this—"

"Rhys, son, you need to come now. Let Rickey take over for you."

I looked at my apprentice and shrugged. "Dad, what's wrong?"

"Come up to the office," he repeated.

I handed the tools to Rickey, who just shrugged. "If you need me, just call, okay?"

Rickey shook his head. He was more than capable, but I was… controlling. That's the word. I laughed at myself and clapped my hand on Rickey's back.

Unfortunately, Dad wanted me in management, and I wanted anything but. So I'd get random urgent calls, and it was never an emergency.

By the time I got to Dad's office, a half hour had passed. I stepped through the door and stopped when I saw Mom. "Um, what's going on?" I asked.

Mom rushed over to me and pulled me into her arms. "I'm so sorry, honey."

"Sorry for what?" I asked, fear gripping me.

Dad came in just then, and when I saw he'd been crying, the alarm bells grew louder.

"Dad, what's going on?"

"It's Helen. She—"

He broke down, and I went to his side to hold him up. "Dad, Aunt Helen is what?"

"She's gone, son. She passed away this morning."

A tidal wave of grief washed over me, and I had a hard time breathing. "No," I lamented as I remembered my beloved aunt and all the years she encircled my family with love. No wonder Mom had driven to the office. She loved Aunt Helen as much as we did, and her divorce from Dad had done nothing to minimize that.

"How?" I finally asked when the wave of grief subsided.

I DROVE WITH Dad to Wilcox while Mom went back to pick up my stepfather, Johney. Dad's wife, Lucy, and my two half sisters would come later. Lucy was only six years older than me. She was smart and funny, and I liked her, though I hadn't at first.

I doted on my very loud twin sisters; they were more like nieces than siblings. We were a family. Even Mom and Johney spent the holidays with us. And Lucy and Mom had grown close and loved to grumble about how impossible Dad was. I think Dad secretly loved being the center of their complaints.

We pulled up at the county funeral home, and I followed Dad up the steps. The elderly man who ran the home met us as soon as we walked in. "Mr. Healy, I'm so sorry for your loss."

He shook Dad's hand and then reached for mine. Why are all funeral directors' hands cold? I inwardly snickered since it was just the sort of thing Aunt Helen would've asked.

Dad followed the director back to the office. Helen hated the place. Even when I lived with her, she'd spent a few days here, mourning lost friends.

Wilcox had changed so much since I was a kid. Aunt Helen's generation was dying off, and the town suffered as a result. Many of the old stores now stood empty. Not much happened here these days, and I knew that had made Aunt Helen sad.

"Your aunt made all her own arrangements, and the funeral is paid for. We just need you to make a few minor decisions about—"

I shut out the conversation. I wasn't ready to make decisions about anything when it came to burying my aunt. "Can I see her?" I interrupted them.

The director nodded once and rose. "Of course. I should've offered first."

I followed them down the hall to a small back room, and inside was one closed casket. The director slowly opened it and revealed my aunt. She had that ugly caked-on makeup that funeral parlors use on corpses. It hurt to see how unnatural she looked, but it also helped me understand that she really was gone.

I put my hand on hers and let the silent tears drip down my face. "I'd, um, I'd like a moment alone with her." Dad put his hand on my shoulder, and when I turned, I saw he was also crying. "Just one moment, Dad. I'd like to say goodbye before it becomes a thing."

He nodded and followed the director out of the room.

"Aunt Helen, why the hell didn't you tell us you were sick?" I asked. Dad told me she'd been dealing with cancer and had kept it a secret. "Yeah, thanks for not answering." I chuckled and could almost hear her laughing as well. "You hated being sick. Still, it would've been nice to have some warning."

I wrapped my fingers around her stiff ones, ignoring that they were lifeless. It didn't matter. She was my aunt—the one person in my life who had always been there for me, for all of us, even my mom.

I sat on one of the seats, let the tears flow freely, and even allowed the sobs to take me. Eventually the worst passed and I reached for the tissues they kindly provided.

I wiped my eyes and stood. "I love you with all my heart, and I always will," I said to the casket.

I turned to walk out, and it felt as if a hand settled on my shoulder. That would be her. Of course she'd find a way to comfort me even after her death. I reached up and put my hand where I felt hers. "Go be at peace, Aunt Helen. We'll hold the fort down here."

I felt a gentle shove—a classic Aunt Helen move. "Well, get a move on, then," she'd have said, and I nodded.

Dad came in behind me, but I'd said my goodbye, and in my mind, she'd also said hers. Aunt Helen had a way of managing things, taking care of us, and making even the worst moments feel right. I was sure her upcoming funeral wouldn't hurt as much after spending those moments with her.

Dad must've had a similar experience, because later, as we sat shoulder to shoulder throughout the service, neither of us cried those deep, painful tears. Clearly, both of us had shed those in private. Aunt Helen had done all she could for us, and now it was our turn to live our best lives.

DAD, LUCY, the girls, and I spent the night at the local B and B where we always stayed when we visited Aunt Helen. The next day Lucy took the kids home while Dad and I walked around the house Aunt Helen had left me in her will. Ever the responsible one, she'd even put it in my name prior to her death. I hadn't known that, but probate could be painful so… I was thankful.

I shook my head and chuckled. "This is such a mess." Dad and I had begged her to let us help with it. He wanted to tear it down and build her a new home—same size but with all the modern conveniences. I'd proposed she move out for a few months, let me gut it and put it to rights once and for all. But she'd refused both of us.

Dad laughed when we heard the will. "That was Aunt Helen saying she liked your idea more than mine." I didn't think he was wrong. She loved the rickety old place. My great-grandfather had bought the home as a kit from Sears and Roebuck back in the 1920s. It was a typical two-story cottage from that time.

My great-grandfather was not a builder, but he built the thing himself. As a result, the walls weren't plumb and the floors were buckled in a few places.

The later addition had fallen down, and Aunt Helen had rebuilt it herself. That was the most structurally sound part of the house. "What a mess," I repeated just as Dad came in behind me.

"You can say that again. At least she hired someone to clean out all her stuff. She was always thoughtful like that," Dad said, sadness crossing his face again. "I wasn't paying attention earlier. What did they do with all her stuff?"

My very efficient aunt had planned everything. Even her stuff was removed before we got to the house. "According to Tim, the attorney, most of it went to charity and her church. Last year she asked what I wanted to keep, and that stuff's in storage someplace out by the interstate."

Dad looked surprised. I knew he thought it strange that I wanted to keep anything, but there were pieces of old furniture I loved—an old flour table, a Hoosier cabinet, and a few other odds and ends. They belonged in the old house.

"You know it's going to cost more to fix this place up than replace it," Dad said, and I just nodded.

"Makes no difference. I'm doing it."

He shook his head. "I figured. You're just like her, you know," he said as he handed me a check. I looked at it and cocked an eyebrow.

"You still use checks?" I asked.

"Don't be a brat," he responded, but he was smiling.

I looked at the amount, and my mouth dropped. "Dad, this is—"

"This is what I set aside years ago to pay for rebuilding this place. It makes sense that, with you doing the work, it should come to you."

"Dad."

He shrugged. "Just make it nice, take your time, and when you're done...."

He looked at me, and I knew he was saying *come back to work*. I shook my head. "Dad, I'm not going to come back."

He sighed, and the pain in his face told me he expected it but didn't like it. "I-I should've kept you close. I shouldn't have pushed you onto your aunt," he said, referencing the time he and Mom were getting divorced. I'd come to live with Aunt Helen then and stayed until graduation—almost four years.

"No, you did exactly what was needed, Dad. It was a lot for a kid to go through, and I needed the stability Aunt Helen provided. You and Mom stood up for me, though." I chuckled at the memories. "Every holiday, every event, you showed up. You didn't abandon me. You gave me what I needed."

Dad nodded. "I never wanted you to feel left out. I... it hurt so much when my parents abandoned me. I didn't want that for you."

"I never felt abandoned. Loved, I always felt loved. Aunt Helen was part of us, always had been."

I drew my dad into a hug. I knew a lot of people my age couldn't hug their fathers, and that made no sense. Mine had always been open to affection. When he pulled back, he wiped away a tear. "Okay, well, you already said you want to do this yourself, so I won't keep you. But son, I-I'd like to come help when I can, it... it'd be healing for me too."

How long you got?" I asked.

He looked at me in a funny way and asked, "Today?"

"Yeah, like right now."

He glanced down at his clothes and smiled. "Demo day?"

I chuckled. We both loved watching the rehab shows on HGTV. You'd think since we did that for a living, it wouldn't be appealing, but what can I say?

Dad grabbed a hammer, ignoring his clean clothes, and I grabbed another. It took all day, but dirty, sweaty, and very happy, we finally pulled all the plaster and lath off the walls and tossed it into the dumpster I had called to be delivered while we worked.

Dad walked around the dust-filled house and shook his head. "It's worse than I thought," he said. Clearly the two-by-fours weren't spaced correctly, and the electrics were a death trap that, luckily, hadn't burned the place down years before. "I'm gonna say one last time—"

I put my hand up to stop him. "Dad, I'll fix it. I want this."

He nodded. "You always knew what you wanted. Okay, well, come on, I'll treat you to a beer, and you can tell me your plans."

I followed him out, but when I turned, the dust swirled in such a way as to make it look like Aunt Helen was standing in the middle of the room. I scrunched up my face. "You were supposed to cross over," I said, and Dad turned and asked what I'd said.

I shook my head. "Just mumbling."

He looked behind me, then at my face again. "She's here?" he asked.

I shrugged. "Probably not, but you know I've always had a good imagination."

He chuckled, but he looked back again. Then he shrugged and walked out and I closed and locked the door behind me. I thought about stopping at the B and B to change, but Wilcox was the kind of town that didn't mind a couple of dirty workmen coming in for a beer, even if we had plaster stuck in our hair.

Dad would be driving back up north, so I knew he wouldn't finish his beer, but it felt good to spend a little time with him. We sat down just as old man Stewie sat across from us. "Hey, boys," he said, and Dad snorted.

"Mr. Stewart, it's nice to see you." I gave my dad a nasty look for his reaction. Cid Stewart—everyone called him Stewie—owned the hardware store in town. Dad and I also thought he and Aunt Helen had a thing going on besides employee and employer. The old man thought of Dad as one of his own, hence the snort.

"It's nice to see you, and a little bird tells me you're redoing your aunt Helen's place. Probably would've done better tearing the thing down, but who am I to say?"

I chuckled. "Let's call it a labor of love," I said, and Stewie's face morphed into grief.

"She did love that old place." We each sipped our beers, letting that thought seep in. Finally Stewie said, "Your aunt left a position open at the hardware store. I didn't want to fill it until I asked if you'd like the job. It's only twenty hours a week, but if you're doing all that work, you might like the employee discount."

I cocked an eyebrow but took another drink before the old man saw it. Did I want to fill my aunt's shoes at the hardware store? I glanced at my father, who had a bemused look on his face. I knew he had some smart remark ready, so that, probably more than anything, made me decide to take the job.

"Sure, Mr. Stewart, I'd be happy to take the job. When do I start?"

The old man's eyebrows lifted, telling me he was as surprised as I was that I'd accepted. "Well, what about tomorrow? Your aunt would come in at nine. She preferred working mornings."

"That sounds great," I said, and when I turned and saw my dad's shocked expression, I laughed. "It'll be fun to get reacquainted with all the locals. It's a good way to do it."

"Indeed it is." Mr. Stewart patted my hand. "Now, I'm going back over here and give you and your dad some time. See you tomorrow," he said cheerfully as he disappeared around the corner.

"What was that?" Dad asked.

"I'm guessing it's Aunt Helen's doing. Knowing her, she told him to hire me if she passed away." We both chuckled at the likely truth of that. "It's all good. I'll enjoy it, and it's just a few hours a week."

Dad shook his head. "You've lost your mind, but whatever makes you happy." He took another sip of beer and stood. "I better get going. Lucy'll have my hide if we get back home to Portland after dark."

I nodded. Dad loved strong women, and there was a reason why Lucy and Mom got along as well as they did. He was smart not to upset the apple cart.

I finished my beer and walked him out. "Come on, I'll drive you back," he said.

"Dad, um, I think I'm going to walk. I need some fresh air after breathing in all the plaster."

He nodded sadly, then leaned over, hugged me again, and got into his car. I'd rented a little house, and I was planning to move in tomorrow, but before I did, I wanted to walk over while it was still light and look around before I fully committed. Lord knows I didn't have time to deal with a bunch of problems with a rental while trying to rehab my aunt's place.

"Okay, well, call if you need anything. Also, your mom and Lucy are planning something for Easter. You should come for that at least."

It was two weeks away, and I knew that was Dad's way of saying he didn't plan to return unless I needed him.

"I'll be there," I said. "Now, get back before you end up in the doghouse."

He waved and smiled, and I watched him drive away.

I loved my parents. I'd been a lucky kid—not only because they loved me, but also because I'd had Aunt Helen to pick up the pieces when they dropped them. I walked down the winding streets, past my little rental, and Aunt Helen's, and onto the old covered bridge that butted up against the property. At one time the bridge had been the main river crossing into town. Now it was blocked to all but foot traffic.

I always came here and dangled my feet through the railings to watch the river flow below. It was my favorite thinking spot.

I'd graduated with my associate degree four years earlier. I was thinking about being a teacher, but only because I had no idea what I really wanted to do. Dad had sat with me at this very spot and asked if I had considered going into the trades. "You'll make a lot more money as an electrician or plumber than you'll ever make as a teacher," he said. "The best part is you get to work with your hands."

I'd always liked helping him redo the homes we lived in while he fixed them up to sell. I hated moving constantly, but I loved the hands-on work. Dad knew that, and his advice had settled on me like a comfortable blanket.

I returned to community college and got licensed as an electrician. It was the best decision I'd ever made.

I was lucky—I had no student loans and I loved what I did. I sighed as I watched the water flow under the bridge. It was strange to be here in Wilcox without my aunt close by. Tearing her house up had been, well, it was hard.

I closed my eyes and whispered, "I love you, Aunt Helen." Then I let the music of the water flowing over the rocks below carry me away.

Xander

I CAME OUT onto the deck—the only part of the ugly house I liked. I'd closed on the thing less than a month ago and already regretted it. Even being on the deck was taking my life in my hands. Whatever blockhead built the house hadn't even used treated lumber.

I glanced over at the covered bridge and chuckled as I remembered the chaos Levi Owens had gotten me into when he convinced me to paint the bridges my ancestors had built over a hundred years before. No surprise there—I usually got into trouble when I was with my besties, Levi and Brandon.

Ms. Helen Healy came to our rescue and had even managed to get a levy placed on the upcoming November ballot to paint and upgrade the bridges in perpetuity.

I sighed as I glanced across the river toward her house, almost directly across from mine. She'd passed away less than a month ago, shortly after I gave her my late great-aunt Greta's journal.

I shook the thought from my head and decided to walk across the bridge. I always planned better when I was on-site.

The sun was low, and the bridge was deep in the shadows of the trees. I loved that someone long ago had thought to plant the gigantic redwood trees. Of course, as beautiful as they were, they'd contributed to the bridge's decline. Moss dotted one side of the structure's roof and sides. If I didn't have the entire city watching my every move, I'd probably apply moss treatment and call it a day.

"You better mind your p's and q's," my mother had lectured me after the commissioner's meeting. She wasn't wrong. I needed to get a lot of new legislation passed if I was going to accomplish my plans.

Mom had fallen off a ladder and broken her ankle last summer. I was somewhere in the middle of Washington at the time and didn't hear about it from her until the next day.

That was it—the freaking last straw. Mom was the only family I had left. I had cousins, but I didn't know them well, and being an out gay man didn't mesh with their religious values. So Mom was all I had, and I sure as hell wouldn't be going off in the wilds in case she ever needed me again.

That's how I ended up living in the ugly monstrosity I now called home. It came with three very developable acres, and everyone in town hated the house, but the lane once boasted five of Wilcox's most beautiful late-Victorian homes.

One after another, investors had stepped in with plans to redo the house and build more like it. But the town council had knocked them all down, again and again.

Would the same thing happen to me? It could. I was native to the area, and I'd fixed up several of the homes in town before I left, but that didn't mean I could fly in and get my way. That's not how my hometown worked.

The fact I'd painted those bridges without the county's permission had met mostly with approval from the residents. Not so much the government officials. They had ignored bridge maintenance and resented that we had shone a light on their inaction. I still had to get approval to build, even if I intended to build houses with historical charm, so I somehow had to make up with the council if that was going to happen.

The inside of the bridge was dark, and I was so deep in thought I didn't notice that I wasn't alone.

I loved to look through the crack between the side of the bridge and the road and watch the river flowing below. I was rushing over to look when I stumbled. "Ouch, fuck," I yelled as I fell.

"Ouch," I heard someone say. "Are you okay? Didn't you see me?"

"Yes, okay, but um, no, I didn't." I got up and turned around, wiping my stinging knee, and looked straight into the face of Rhys Healy. "Oh, um, sorry, I really didn't see you there."

"Obviously," he said as he stood up. "You sure you're okay?"

"Oh, yeah, thanks. Um, I didn't know you were still in town."

He was in the shadows, but I saw a sad smile cross his face. "Yeah, I started renovating Aunt Helen's house today. I'm moving back."

"Oh yeah? Cool," I said, and Rhys walked me the rest of the way across the bridge.

We came out into the light, and I barely managed not to drool. Rhys Healy had grown up nicely. He was at least six inches shorter than me, probably more, and his thin frame was bound tight with muscles that his tight-fitting, albeit dirty, clothes didn't hide.

"You weren't joking," I said, smiling, hoping to get him to do the same.

He looked down at his clothes and rewarded me with a smile. God, he was so handsome.

"Well, I was just going to take a walk through town. You... you wanna join me?"

Rhys shook his head. "No, I was just taking a break. I need to shower 'cause I'll be doing the same thing tomorrow morning. There's a lot to do."

I remembered the state of Ms. Healy's home when I visited before she died. "Yeah, I, you know, I do rehab work too."

Rhys smiled again. "Yeah, I remember. Okay, well, I'll see you around," he said, and then he veered left into a smaller house.

I walked on into town, thinking about Rhys. He was a freshman in high school when I was a senior—too young for me at the time, but damn, I'd noticed him even then.

I turned up the street and into the town I'd fallen more in love with after I left than I was when I lived here. Hell, my family's roots were almost as deep as the Healys'. I had a stake in this game. Even if I wasn't as influential as Helen Healy had been, I hoped I'd be able to pull on my family legacy to help.

I sighed as I surveyed the empty storefronts I passed. Wilcox was slowly dying. I'd begun my career here, but since then my business had flourished. I went from renovating the homes here to helping run a commercial company that built all over Oregon, California, and Washington. Interstate 5 was their only requirement.

It'd been five years since I moved to Portland, and I missed my hometown. Yeah, it was great having guys to date, and Wilcox sure as hell didn't have many. I'd exchanged home for easy access to booty calls. At least, that's what my buddies kept telling me. They weren't wrong. I liked men. I liked men a lot.

Rhys Healy. All I knew was the man was sex on legs. Fuck me, the guy was probably straight, but I didn't usually feel an attraction for straight men. I was a total sucker for a sexy gay dude—pun totally intended.

I should've told him I was sorry about his aunt's passing. Instead I all but swallowed my damned tongue.

I shook off the thoughts of the cute ass I'd seen as he walked away and remembered why I'd come into town. I needed to get the town behind my idea to improve its infrastructure.

Having worked as a commercial developer for half a decade, I knew we needed to create a town plan before the developers found us. Hell, if I played my cards right, *I'd* be the developer and could control that myself.

We were one of the last towns to get attention, being a bit too far south of the big cities, but that's where the covered bridges came into play. We could use their quaint aesthetics to attract people who were hungry for small towns, had jobs that could support them here, and could contribute to the local economy.

I looked back at the bridge where I'd stumbled on Rhys earlier. I was convinced the bridges were the draw. I knew they were. I just needed to keep pressure on the county and the town to follow through on their plan to fix them. Inadvertently, I glanced back at the small house Rhys had entered.

The sun was just beginning to set, and it wouldn't do for me to plow over another Wilcox citizen, so I turned back and headed toward my own monstrosity. As I walked by, I forced myself not to stare at the house I knew the sexy man inhabited. Instead I studied Ms. Healy's old home—the one Rhys was gutting. I knew, mostly from town gossip, that he had gone to work with his dad, doing some sort of construction.

I wondered if there was a chance we could hook up… or something.

I forced myself not to think of the "or something." I needed hookups, not relationships. My luck with men was, well, abysmal. If I was going to succeed in Wilcox, I shouldn't create problems because I sucked at relationships. I'd just have to enjoy Rhys from a distance. That was the smart thing to do.

I had to bump the door of my house to get it unstuck, and when it finally gave way, I walked in and sighed at the ugly architecture. Its one redeeming quality was that it was only a few hundred feet from the covered landmark. In my mind I could see the new homes this side of the bridge. If I could fix what someone else had broken, it might help to persuade the council to accept my plans to rebuild Wilcox's commercial properties. That felt important.

The image of the handsome Rhys Healy came to mind, and I shook my head. "Don't screw yourself just as you're getting started," I chastised, but then I chuckled. I knew I was terrible at relationships, but I also knew that if Rhys were ever amenable, I'd jump right into bed with him, even if it hurt my plans.

Rhys

I HAD TO look down to avoid my new boss seeing me smile. "My name is Stewie, and I expect you to call me that."

He told me that he felt old when people called him Mr. Stewart. I'd been calling him that for years, but that was when Aunt Helen was alive. I guess even he knew she wouldn't tolerate me not using his proper name.

Stewie was funny and charming, and I assumed the two had been an item, at least after he was widowed. Stewie told me over and over how my aunt had taken him under her wing after his wife died over three decades ago.

Knowing Aunt Helen, she kept a firm barrier between them. That's just how my aunt operated. She was loving, kind, open, and generous, but when it came to her life, she didn't let anyone control it—not even my father or me.

"Now, for any work you need on that house, you call that Louis boy. I know he looks like he's tweaking on something, but trust me, he's not. He's a solid worker. Oh, and Jeffrey. He's as old as the hills—almost as old as me—but don't let that fool you. He can do the work of three men half his age. Besides, Jeffrey knows young Louis and can rein him in if he needs to."

That's how Stewie instructed me the first day I came to work at the hardware store, and that helped me more than any money he could pay me. I loved the house and fully intended to do as much of the work as possible, but I also understood that I couldn't do it all myself, and I sure didn't want to ask Dad to send crews from his jobsite just to help me with my house.

Dad and I had already removed most of the interior. With Louis and Jeffrey's help, we quickly removed the old, crappy siding, got the structure up to code, and replaced the cladding with a newer version.

Unfortunately, I hadn't paid attention to the foundation, which was my first mistake of many more to come, but once I was sure it was secure enough, I had the house jacked up and a brand-new basement foundation poured.

"How the hell is this place still standing?" Jeffrey asked as he pulled his cap off and scratched his head.

"Dude, did you not know Aunt Helen? Not even a house would dare fall down when she was in charge."

Old Jeffrey laughed out loud. "Your aunt was one of the sweetest people I ever met, but cross her and she would put you in your place fast enough," he said. I had to smile. God, I missed her.

It took over a week to secure the structure and pour the new concrete walls. I hadn't planned on using the basement as a living space, but it meant I could put in windows to code and open up the back of the house. I also ensured the basement would never leak, unlike the old basement under Aunt Helen's home. So, despite the headache, it was a good thing in the end.

But I was thankful my father had given me money, because all these renovations were quickly becoming expensive.

Once the structure was secure, I had the guys strip the rest of the plaster. The electrical was scary, to say the least. I was surprised the house hadn't burned to the ground, so I wanted to wire it correctly the moment I had the city's approval. I knew from experience that a worksite needed to be weatherproof first, and it needed working electrics. Luckily, the guys did most of the demo while I worked at the hardware store.

Stewie hadn't been wrong when he told me Jeffrey was one of the best workers around and that he kept the young guy's nose to the grindstone.

I walked through the cleaned-out structure and sighed. "Jeez, Aunt Helen, this really was a mess."

I felt an imaginary pop to the back of my head—a muscle memory of something she'd have done had I said that when she was alive. I just laughed.

"So, you're keeping an eye on things?" I didn't expect an answer, but I suspected she was still watching over things. That woman adored the house. "Well, I know you aren't liking that I'm gutting it, but when it's done, you'll be proud. I promise."

I knew I was being silly, but a feeling of peace washed over me, and it felt like she approved. Not that it mattered. The house had to be fixed or dozed. I shuddered to think what her ghost, if it really were here, would've done to me if I'd knocked it down.

I was about to leave when I heard a knock at the door. I caught a whiff of coffee and the homemade cookies Aunt Helen always put out when expecting company. It made the hackles on the back of my neck rise. Maybe I was taking the whole "Aunt Helen hadn't passed over" thing a little too seriously.

When I pulled the door open and found the handsome Xander Petterson standing in front of me, I laughed. My nosy-ass aunt would totally be playing matchmaker, and I seriously doubted the grave could keep her from that.

He cocked an eyebrow, and I shrugged. "Sorry. I wasn't expecting company. Come on in."

"Um, sorry to interrupt, but Mom saw you working over here and sent me with this," he said as he handed me a pie.

"Your mother baked me a pie?" I asked, and he shrugged.

"She bakes everyone a pie. If you're sick, you get chicken noodle soup. If you're sad, you get fried chicken. If you're moving into a new home, you get pie."

"She knows I'm not moving in and I lived here before, right?" I asked.

"Yeah, probably, but hey, it's pecan. Wanna share?"

"Well, not here in the construction filth," I said as I led him out of the house and across to the rental.

The rental house was only five hundred square feet, and it was adequate for me alone. But Xander was a big man, well over six feet, probably more like six three or four. His shoulders fit perfectly in the door frame. Any bigger and he sure as hell wouldn't have fit.

I had to force myself not to bump against him. Not that I minded. Xander Petterson was a fine piece of manness.

I cut us both a slice, thankful he parked his hot body on the stool on the other side of the kitchen peninsula from me. When I took a bite, I couldn't resist the moan. "Damn, that's good."

I looked up just as Xander swallowed hard. Shit, okay, well, clearly he liked guys. Straight men don't look at you like he was looking at me. Damn, I bet he tasted as sweet as the pie.

I shook my head to force my thoughts away from the places that I could stick my tongue to taste him. "So, your mom," I said and lingered on that topic, hoping to cool shit down. I liked men, and Xander was totally my type, but shit, I wasn't looking to hook up with a local, much less the town fucking superhero.

"Yeah, so she cooks pies," Xander said, and I couldn't help but laugh.

"Pies. Anyway, so you're moving back to town?" I said, hoping to push us onto a different subject before I did something I'd regret.

Just then, his phone rang. For a split second, he didn't look at it. Instead he continued to look at me in that hungry way. Then he glanced down. "Shit, hold on, I need to take this." He stood up and walked the four steps to the front door.

"Hey, yeah, what's going on now?" he asked, and I watched his face drop.

"Okay, let me get back home and I'll call you back."

He hung up and turned toward me. "I'm sorry, work."

I smiled and thanked him for the pie. He looked at his uneaten slice, then back at me, and he gave me another look of regret for leaving a piece of delicious pie on his plate.

"Maybe I can come by later?" he said, but his phone dinged with a message.

"Shit, okay, I'll… I'll see you around," he said, and I followed him out the front door. I watched him leave as he called whoever texted him. Xander was one of those bodybuilder types who had a V-shaped body that spilled down onto an absolutely perfect bubble butt ass.

I thought that's exactly where I'd be licking. Then I shook my head and went back into the house.

I ate the rest of my pie, put Xander's back in the dish, covered it, and slipped it into my refrigerator.

I didn't have the same build as Xander, and even if I worked out daily, I never would. Not only that, I had to watch what I ate or I'd get the same pot belly my father sported.

I cleaned up, full from the pie and able to forgo supper. Then I slipped into the shower and washed away the dirt of the day. Xander's expression as he'd looked at me filled my mind, and I couldn't help but imagine what it would feel like to have his huge hands moving up and down my body.

I moaned as I imagined his cock lining up to my backside and him looking at me as he fucked me from above. I came with images of that in mind.

"Fuck," I said as the water washed away my ecstasy. That would probably be a bad idea, but I knew for a fucking fact that if Xander hadn't been called away, I would've ended up showing the man my bed and a hell of a lot more. I wasn't sure whether that was a really great idea or an epically bad one.

Regardless, if he came around again, it was probably inevitable that I would find out.

OKAY, SO maybe I was just pathetic. I kept watching for Xander to return, hoping to get to know him a bit more, and by "getting to know him," I meant "fuck around." Unfortunately, I didn't see him for weeks.

Once the city approved me to keep going and I was convinced the house wouldn't fall in, I rewired the entire place from the basement up. I knew the roof would have to be replaced, and I dreaded it, but I wanted to wait until the rainy season was over.

I'd removed as many of the interior walls on the first floor as possible. The old 1920s style was way out of fashion, and although I loved the idea of keeping the house as original as possible, I also wanted a modern living space. So, after the foundation was done, I spent the next few weeks with Johney, who was an architect. He helped me design the place to maximize the space and talked me into tearing off Aunt Helen's addition and building a proper one onto the back. That enlarged the master bedroom on the second floor. It also gave me a beautiful kitchen and dining area overlooking the yard and river. I could imagine a big deck on the back and landscaping that would maximize the river access.

The renovation kept me busy, but that didn't mean I didn't have enough downtime not to think about getting some of my other needs met.

Shit, I needed to go to town or something, but I tried to force myself to focus on what was in front of me. Aunt Helen had left me with one thing I'd never lose—the need to protect and hold our history close, which meant preserving things like her house.

Preserve, yes. Keep old and limited, no. With Johney's help, I added a pergola to the side of the house from the basement level. I was a single man in a world that was overcast and cold half the year. I needed a damned hot tub if I was going to live here.

We built the hot tub with access to a bathroom in the new basement, and the change made it much more appealing. My goal was to turn the basement into a sort of man cave. The upstairs would be more formal, while the basement could be out of sight, and I could have my big leather sectional and big-screen TV down there without my mom looking disapprovingly every time she came over. Not that I expected her to come that often. Still, I had the space, so why not use it?

Aunt Helen must've approved, since I hadn't felt her since the night Xander undressed me with his fucking eyes. Damn, why did I keep reliving that?

Dad and the girls showed up that weekend to give Lucy a break. We didn't get much done, but we enjoyed watching the girls run around searching for bugs and whatever else six-year-olds look for.

"This reminds me of when you were little," Dad said, nostalgia falling over him.

"I imagine it reminds you of when you were little too," I said, which made him smile.

"I moved in with Aunt Helen when I was their age. Maybe a little younger. I was depressed, so Aunt Helen took me down to the river and showed me all the frogs and bugs and stuff. When she mentioned they used to pan for gold in the river, I was hooked."

"Really? You never told me all this."

He reached over and patted my knee. "Son, one of my biggest regrets is that I didn't make more time when you were young. I know Aunt Helen kept all the panning stuff. I saw it in the basement not long ago, but, well—"

He paused, and I glanced over. "Dad, don't go beating yourself up. I would've hated panning in that cold river. Remember when you tried to get me to go swimming?"

He snorted. "Okay, that does make me feel better."

The girls ran over and excitedly showed Dad a ladybug they'd found. They quoted some book about grouchy ladybugs that their teacher must've read to them, and then they ran off to free it.

Dad stood up and turned. "I'm so thankful you didn't listen to me and you're turning this place into a good home. Aunt Helen was right. We need to keep it in the family."

As he wandered toward the girls, I was left to my thoughts. I loved it here, always had. Being a working member of the town made me love Wilcox that much more.

Folks always came into the hardware store and asked about Dad and the girls. Not often Mom or Lucy, but they didn't know them. Very few people who came in didn't comment on the progress with Aunt Helen's house. "She'd be so proud of you for all you're doing," they'd say, but then they'd share valuable gossip about what was happening in town.

I'd never been one for gossip. I always thought it was just small-town chatter and not worth listening to. Now that I lived here, I was beginning to understand why it was so important. Decisions that affected us as a town were always being bounced around.

It only took a while for me to realize that the gossip was the same as a town hall meeting. Decisions were made long before the town council met. If anything new popped up, you could bet it'd be voted out. Not because it was a bad idea but because the townspeople hadn't had time to talk it out, think about it, or sometimes yell at each other.

According to the town gossip, Xander and his buddy Levi, a guy I hadn't seen in years, got into trouble for painting a couple of the old covered bridges where Levi lived. My aunt must've been involved too, although no one went into detail about that.

Now the town was talking about the old covered bridges in our county getting a much-needed facelift. I heard that my aunt had convinced the town to put a levy to maintain the bridges on the next ballot.

I was all for that. The bridge by my house wasn't horrible, but the paint was peeling, That was to be expected, and I liked it looking worn, but I knew it wouldn't do to let it sit for long like that.

Unfortunately, by the time summer hit, the conversations shifted from fixing up the bridges to how much property the town needed to set aside on each side of the bridge next to me. Of course, folks knew I owned the land on my side of the bridge, but no one ever mentioned that. I guessed the folks were talking in front of me on purpose, to test the waters.

They could test all they wanted. I wasn't going to donate or sell my land. Aunt Helen had made it clear it needed to stay in our family, and I felt exactly the same.

That didn't mean I wouldn't be willing to carve out a few feet on my side of the bridge to make public access easier. Just not all of it. And I didn't want a bunch of people around the area anyway. We already had a couple of nice parks in town, and both needed a lot of improvement. The last thing I wanted was for another park to fall into disrepair next to my home.

All that aside, I listened intently to any mention of Xander Petterson. He seemed to have gone MIA. I had caught glimpses of him in town, rushing in and out, but I never had a chance to catch up with him.

He could be avoiding me, but it wasn't like I came on to him. If anything, he was doing the coming on… but it didn't matter. He was a freaking model-looking sexy Nordic god with a mane of auburn hair and a tanned body, which was a strange combination. Most men with his hair coloring were super fair-skinned. The look made him way too hot for someone like me.

Xander probably dated supermodels, and I was a lowly electrician. I loved the choices I'd made for my career, and I wouldn't ever regret it, but I wasn't the type for a man like Xander Petterson. For what had to be the millionth time, I forced away my thoughts of him.

When it was clear we'd finally entered the dry season, I called Dad. "So, I think it's time. Can you lend me your roofing crew for a few days? I'd prefer to jerk that roof off and have it back on just in case we end up with a storm we aren't prepared for."

He agreed and told me to let him know when I was ready. True to his word, the crew showed up that Monday, ripped off the roof, and had it rebuilt before the weekend rains hit. I'd just gotten home from the hardware store and rushed over to ensure we hadn't sprung a leak when I ran into Xander Petterson.

"Wow, sorry. We seem to keep meeting here," I said. He smiled, and fuck me, that man had a fucking dimple. How had I not noticed he had a fucking dimple? I was so dead.

I glanced up and straight into his bright green eyes. For a moment my legs felt weaker than they should. Damn, why did I react like that?

"I just got back and thought, well, you know, I've got a property just across the river. Mind joining me for dinner?"

I looked at him, surprised. Was he asking me to go over to his place? "Um." I looked down at my dirty clothes. I'd been helping Stewie rearrange the back room to reopen it as a feed store.

"Maybe, but not tonight," I said, silently yelling at myself for being so stupid. I hadn't gotten laid in months, not to mention the fact that I'd fantasized about fucking this very man since I'd last seen him.

"Next time," he said and smiled. I watched as he disappeared back across the bridge; then I had to run to the rental before the rains started again.

So, Xander Petterson had just asked me for a hookup. I had to let that settle. I guess I had some sense of self-preservation. I could use the release, but I lived here, and he was the town's sweetheart. *No, I did the right thing*, I thought, even though I didn't believe that in the least.

Xander

I KNEW THE moment the words were out of my mouth what it sounded like. Two gay men in a small town who barely knew each other, and one asking the other over for dinner? Yeah, that sounded like a hookup.

Rhys had turned me down. That was good. I mean, I'd been thinking of doing some intense things to him since the last time we'd spoken. My God, even now, thinking of how he moaned when he took a bite of that pie....

I shivered as I thought about hearing him make that sound around my cock. *Damn, shake that shit off.* But it was so hard. He was every ounce my type—he was smart, liked working with his hands, and had a small but tightly built frame. If I were to pursue anything with him, it wouldn't be a one-time thing. I could be wrong, but he gave off relationship vibes. Not sure why I thought that—maybe because I'd known his aunt, maybe because I knew he was attached to Wilcox. But did I want that? I shook my head, unsure and embarrassed. "Smooth operator," I said to the room, and the deluge that followed me inside seemed to agree with my sarcasm.

I had told Councilman Max about my plan to tear down my home and build more suitable houses in its place. I knew the guy couldn't keep his mouth shut to save his life, but of all the council members, he was the least likely to say no. His father had been on the council before him, and some digging in our local archives told me he had been most upset with the ugly '90s house.

The bridge was part of that plan. I wanted it repainted and a small section of land designated as a park so people could enjoy the structure. Hopefully, tourists would come to Wilcox to spend money. If we wanted a commercial downtown, we had to have something to interest visitors.

I'd walked over the bridge today to look at the land around it when I spotted Rhys.

My dinner invitation had initially been to test the boundaries about him selling land to the city for a park on his side of the river. I owned the land on my side of the bridge, and I could and would donate part of that for the park. But the Healy side was closest to town. Ideally, we'd need some land on his side to make it work.

From my discreet questions, I knew the Healys held on to the land in that area like a dragon hoarded treasure. More than a few people had tried to get Rhys's aunt to sell the land for development, and more than a few people were quickly and decisively rebuffed.

In the late '80s, one developer proposed forcing her to sell through eminent domain. He'd been unceremoniously sent packing.

But on the day I took my aunt Greta's journal to her, she hadn't stood proud. Instead, she looked lost and sad. She clearly loved Wilcox, but how much had she sacrificed for it? Too much, I suspected.

I didn't know Rhys well, but considering he was redoing a home that should've been torn down and replaced, I had to suspect he wasn't much different from his aunt. He wouldn't want to part with much land for the bridge, but maybe he'd part with a little. But I'd have to figure out a better way to talk to him, at least where I didn't sound like I wanted to get into his pants.

I chuckled as I popped open a beer and sat on the sofa that Mom insisted I get when she saw that my place was still empty, even over a month after I purchased it.

I couldn't convince Rhys Healy I didn't want to get into his pants when I was this attracted to him. I'd have to devise a different strategy to talk him out of a bit of land for the bridge project. I set the beer down and lay back on the sofa. What would it hurt to actually date someone, I wondered.

Rhys was special; I could tell that. I wasn't in town often, so if it didn't work out, it's not like we'd see each other. I was surprised to realize I didn't want just a hookup. Not with him.

Recently I'd been thinking about forever, especially when I looked at Brandon and his new love, Cliff, and at Levi and Keya and their gorgeous baby girl that none of us, not even me, could get enough of.

I probably wasn't created for a relationship that lasted forever. I wasn't selfish, per se. In fact, I'd been taught from an early age to be generous. "Don't you ever think yourself above anyone else, Xander," my beloved aunt Greta repeatedly told me. "You never know when you're going to be in the same situation as those you're looking down on. Count your blessings and make sure you're bestowing them on others."

I missed her. She had kept me solid when I was a kid. Mom loved her as much as me, and we both depended on her until she died. Now it was a hard pill to swallow, knowing that she died of a broken heart.

Maybe that was my problem—I was too much like Aunt Greta. Even after she tried to love another person, she ended up with a total loser who milked her dry and cast her aside. She'd come back to Wilcox broken and died a short time later. I wasn't keen on finding that kind of love or falling for someone I'd never be able to get over.

It was ironic that I found Helen's nephew so desirable. No, I wasn't a relationship kind of guy, but that didn't mean it didn't have some appeal.

Such as right now. It'd be delightful to have a sexy man—very much like the one across the bridge—snuggled comfortably in my arms.

I fell asleep dreaming of the handsome Rhys and woke up early in the morning sore from sleeping on the lumpy couch.

I smiled at the memory of my dreams. Yeah, all reservations aside, Rhys Healy could be really fun to get to know better.

Rhys

"CONGRATULATIONS, BOY, we can't wait to see it when you're done." That was pretty much what everyone said as soon as the roof was replaced. Where before, I'd have blown the compliment off, now it felt like the town was going through the process with me. They truly were pleased to see my progress.

It took another two months before I could sheetrock the place. I was nearing the finish line and was freaking excited about it. I'd seen Xander several times since the hookup proposition, but never when we could talk. I'd already decided that if he asked again, I'd accept. What did I have to lose? It's not like I'd be making the town like me less. If anything, they'd relish something new to gossip about.

I'd already had to make a trip out of town to satisfy *the needs*, as I was calling my occasional booty trips. Having someone close would cut down on a lot of wasted time and money. Unfortunately, the man was stupidly busy and never in the same place I was.

So nothing happened. Things got even crazier when Stewie ended up in the hospital with a heart issue right after I got the sheetrock up. Since I was the only other person working at the hardware store, it fell to me to keep things running. Luckily I had the guys to help me, or the entire build would've come to a screeching halt.

When I finally got to the finishes, I was ecstatic. I'd worked so hard to make it happen that it would've consumed my life if it hadn't been for the hardware store.

Now that I was so close to completing the house, I wanted to be there when it was painted and my kitchen and bathrooms went in.

I didn't mind the tiny rental, but I was ready to have my own space, and Aunt Helen's house was going to be spectacular. I hadn't felt her presence in a while, and that, more than anything, confirmed it was no longer just Aunt Helen's house. It was becoming mine.

Stewie ended up with a stent and a forceful admonishment from his doctor to stay off his feet for a few weeks. So, because I liked him and was beginning to treasure the store's value to the community, I convinced him to stay seated on the stool up front at the register. I spent the next few weeks after his surgery diving into projects I knew needed doing in the store, even if that meant I didn't have time to work on my place.

I'd just finished cleaning a back room when I came out front and once again ran right into Xander Petterson. "Sorry," I said, resisting the urge to say something about running into him again… literally.

He looked at me with that slow smile of his and winked. "Someone's been doing some deep cleaning," he said, and I looked down at my cobweb-covered clothes.

"Yeah, trying to get some work done while I'm here full-time. What brings you in?" I asked.

"Looking for a fuse," he said. "I blew one this morning and didn't want to wait for it to come through the mail."

I cocked my eyebrow. The worst enemies of local business are large online stores, but I didn't respond to the delivery comment. Instead, I asked what kind of fuse he needed.

Of course we had it. Several, in fact. I showed him where they were and left him to it. A few moments later, he showed up at the front desk.

"Um," I heard him say behind me. I pasted a smile on my face as I turned, even though I hated to talk to customers when I was busy. "So, I wondered, would you maybe like to go have dinner with me, or maybe lunch?" He blushed in such a cute way that my *don't bother me while I'm working* heart melted a bit.

"Oh, I… well… um."

"Yes, yes, he will," Stewie said behind me. I turned and gave him the stink eye, which just made the old man snicker.

"*Mister* Stewart, I can answer for myself, thank you."

He just laughed again and ignored me.

"Yeah, I guess that's okay, but you know, I'm not really looking for a relationship," I said.

Xander cocked an eyebrow but smiled. "I wasn't proposing marriage, just a friendly get-together."

I blushed. I don't know why I kept flubbing up stuff with him. I nodded and swallowed hard, trying to get the knot out of my throat. "Yeah, that'd be fine. Just, you know, call me sometime."

He smiled, took his fuse, and disappeared out the front door. I turned to my boss and put my hands on my hips. "Listen, old man—"

He put his hand up to stop me. "No, you listen. I chased after your sweet aunt for three decades, and she kept me at arm's length. I've been watching you for the past few months, and you're just like her. I might not have been able to influence your stubborn aunt, but I can influence you. Xander Petterson is a good guy. You're a good guy too. Don't throw away a chance of getting to know each other better."

He made sense, and I knew he wasn't wrong. Of course, that was the first time he out and out admitted he and Aunt Helen were involved, which struck me as important. I still did my best to give him a look. Then I *hmph*ed, which even to me sounded just like my aunt, and walked back to the room I'd been working on earlier. The dust had settled enough that I could get the mop out and hopefully finish most of it.

There were a lot of rooms in the back, and Stewie had at least another few weeks before he could be here on his own again. So I had plans for horse equipment and a chicken center, along with cooking and canning supplies.

I'd been in a lot of hardware stores over the years and knew this one had a lot of potential—good potential since it was meeting so many different needs. What we didn't need were old rooms filled with junk.

I came back up front an hour later to see Stewie staring at his phone. "Hey, boss, what's up?" I asked.

He quickly put his phone down, which made me suspicious. "Okay, spill," I said.

"Well, you forgot to give that young lad your phone number."

"Wait, did you just send my number to Xander?"

He smiled. "Remember, I'm the boss."

"You're a scoundrel, is what you are," I said, but I couldn't be angry with him. I'd learned to think of Stewie as a friend—a very nosy, very boundaryless friend. I hadn't forgotten to give my number to Xander. I'd just figured if he were really interested, he would ask.

"Well, don't hold your breath. I'm not expecting him to call, text, or anything, and you better not push the issue with him either, or I'll leave you here with all this dust and mess to manage on your own."

Stewie put his hands up, but he smiled. "I've done what I'm gonna do. It's up to you young bucks to figure it out from here."

I snorted and shook my head. "Okay, whatever. I'm headed home. Are you okay with closing up on your own?"

"Right as rain," he said and waved me off. He was doing a lot better, and the townsfolk tended to show up later in the day to ensure he stayed that way.

At least his weekend help would give me the time I needed to paint the rest of the house. I thought about the hardware store as I jogged the mile home, and I was surprised at how much I was enjoying it.

I was a licensed electrician and could make more money in a month than the store probably made in a year, but the store was a hub for the community. I guessed Stewie's kids were on the verge of forcing him to retire.

I couldn't blame them. It was getting to the point where I was concerned about leaving him there, even for a few hours on his own. If I could figure out how to own the store and hire help to run it, I could still do contract work around town. That'd keep the income flowing and the old store open.

My birthday weekend arrived, and I hadn't given it much thought. When Mom, Johney, Dad, Lucy, and the twins showed up, I was stunned. Everyone grabbed paint rollers and brushes and began painting, while Mom volunteered to watch the girls.

My mother was a lot of things, but handy wasn't one of them. I'll never understand why she married a carpenter and created an electrician, only to then marry an architect.

It didn't take long before most of the rooms were painted. But painting is mostly a solitary sport, and as I poured the soft yellow paint I was using for the first floor into my tray, I thought about Stewie again. *Me the owner of a hardware store. Wouldn't that be the shit?* I didn't need to worry about it yet, and I needed to focus on getting the paint on these walls. My custom kitchen and bathroom cabinets would be ready in the next week or so, and once those were in, I could turn the water on, get the final approval from the city for occupancy, and move in—all before fall hit, if I was lucky.

When Jenny came over and sat beside me, I knew she had something on her mind. As usual, she didn't say anything until Chelsie joined her. Sure enough, as soon as Chelsie sat down, Jenny asked, "So, are you never coming home?"

"Yeah, I'll come visit more when the house is done," I said.

"No, dummy," Chelsie said, and I gave her the stink eye. "We want to know if you are ever *moving* back home."

I chuckled. "You're a brat, and you're lucky I love you. Dummy indeed," I said as I went back to painting the wall. "This is my house now, so no, I probably won't move back to your house. But you can always come here to visit," I assured them.

"Why did Aunt Helen give you the house?" Chelsie asked.

I shrugged. "She wants us to have our roots," I said, and both girls looked at me in a funny way.

I laughed. "Okay, hold on." I poured the rest of the paint back into the paint bucket. "Come with me." I led the way down to the river. "Do you see that tree?" Both girls nodded. "Okay, do you see the roots sticking out of the ground?"

"Yeah," Jenny said.

"Well, families are like trees. We have imaginary roots growing beneath us. The Healys, you two, Dad, and I have roots that grow deep in the soil of Wilcox. But you see that tree down there?" I pointed toward a tree that had toppled over. "That one fell when the river eroded the soil from around its roots." I sat on a boulder next to where we were standing and waited for the girls to join me.

"Aunt Helen was afraid that, with all of us leaving Wilcox, we'd be like that tree that fell. She wanted me to fix up her old house so when you two or Dad wanted to come home, you could and, you know, be back where your roots run deep again."

The girls didn't say anything, which always indicated that they were processing what I'd said. Then they got up at the same time—another weird twin skill—and headed back toward the house. "Hey, where are you going?" I asked.

Chelsie turned around, smiling. "We're going to go help paint our roots."

I groaned and smiled. Until then we had managed to keep the girls occupied with other stuff to prevent them from wanting to help with the painting, knowing the mess they would make. Oh well, I thought as I looked across the river and saw the poor tree with its roots exposed. I'd rather clean up paint spills and have the girls feel like my home was theirs than worry about things being perfect. Which, for me, was a big deal. I liked my work to be spot-on.

I got up, still smiling, and followed the girls in. I'd already decided which room would be theirs and had picked a light lavender color for the walls. Might as well let them get started on that. It wasn't like they could do too much damage. Hell, I still needed to put up the trim around the windows.

When I showed the girls the paint, they were excited, and I didn't even complain when they drew pictures instead of painting. Luckily, Lucy came in and took them off my hands before it got too crazy.

I finished the room and put the paint away just as Dad and Johney came in carrying pizza. "Did you drive up to Eugene for this?" I asked, knowing these weren't the local pizza boxes.

"Oh yeah, it's worth the drive, don't you think?" Johney asked.

I laughed. "Oh yeah, Wilcox is an amazing place, but the restaurants here suck."

"Hey," Mom said as she came in behind me. "You might be correct, but you should watch your mouth."

We all chuckled but didn't argue. On a construction site, *suck* wasn't even considered a cuss word.

I watched my family, who'd all come down to support me for my birthday, and knew tomorrow, my actual birthday, would be a day with nothing happening on the house. I knew the rituals, and they included overeating, lots of laughter, and drinking the night away once the girls were put to bed.

I didn't mind. Most of the house was painted—much more than I'd have gotten done if it were just me. At least I could enjoy my birthday without working.

Xander

I'D BEEN running like a crazy person since I'd last seen Rhys. My company had taken on a fast-food project just south of the California border, and it was a pain in my ass.

The entire thing was taking up most of my life, and I'd just gotten things back on track when I got home. Of course, the ugly house met me with more problems—over half the lights wouldn't work. I really did need to tear the piece of crap down and rebuild.

I admit I looked for Rhys when I entered the store. Mom told me he'd been taking on more hours since old man Stewie had a heart issue. I expected to see the old man there. In all my years growing up, I'd never not seen Stewie in the store.

I walked around until I heard someone working in the back. I was trying to build up the courage to talk to him when Rhys burst out of the room and all but knocked me down. Of course, I bumbled it all.

I was a successful businessman; I handled people for a living. I had dated men up and down the Pacific Northwest, and I couldn't even ask a guy I liked out on a date without totally bumbling it.

If it weren't for old man Stewie, I'd have walked away with nothing. In fact I did walk away with nothing, not even his number. What the hell was wrong with me?

I was headed over to Mom's when I heard my phone ping. I needed gas, so I pulled into Carter's Store, and while the attendant filled my tank, I glanced down. Stewie had texted me. I wasn't sure how he got my number, but I had to guess it was my mom's doing since she was in everyone's business.

The old man had texted me Rhy's number. I laughed out loud and texted Stewie back. *Yeah, thanks for that.*

I didn't get a reply, so I paid for the gas and headed to Mom's.

I had just parked when I got the next ping on my phone, and I smiled, anticipating some remark from Stewie. But it was my assistant texting *911.*

"Shit," I said out loud. I expected to hear the union guys in California had walked out on the project again, but when I called, my assistant answered.

"Boss, how long would it take you to get to Rainmore?"

I forced myself to remember the particulars of the Rainmore, Washington, project. My company was doing a contract with the lumber mill there.

"What's going on?" I asked, resigned.

"The mill caught fire, and the owner is about to shit his pants. He wants us to bring in crews and fix it before he starts losing money."

"How bad is the damage?"

"Owner says bad, but not something we can't fix."

I snorted. "Yeah, that's what they all say." I checked my watch; Rainmore was a good four hours away, and I needed to check on Mom first. "I'll head up there in a bit, but you tell Sam, the owner, he needs to meet me there when I arrive. I need to know what I'm dealing with. Meanwhile, make sure they can afford to pay us."

"Got it, boss. I'll make sure he understands."

Mom was fine. She hugged me, made a couple of sandwiches for me to eat along the way, and sent me packing like she did whenever I had to run out on our time together.

I was tired of the rat race, and I'd only been in it for a short time. I wanted to come home and reinvest in the future there. If I played my cards right—and God, I hope I did—I'd be able to make things work so I was no longer chasing money up and down Interstate 5. I was ready to be home and to stay that way.

When Rhys came to mind, I forced myself to ignore it, even though I sure as hell wanted to taste his sexy little body.

Rhys

I TRIED NOT to get my feelings hurt. Xander had taken my number and then disappeared. I hadn't seen him in weeks, and it was hard not to imagine that he was avoiding me. And he'd come into my place of employment and chased me, right?

No matter. I was busy enough. I finished the house just in time for the autumn rains, and the hot tub was installed right before I moved in. Damn, I was so ready. I accidentally let slip while speaking with Polly at work that I was ready to move in, and the next thing I knew, she and Xander's mom had organized an open house. I had no intention of having an open house, but I wasn't strong enough to resist.

When I should've been soaking in my hot tub, enjoying the changing leaves, I was serving canapés to the town as they traipsed dirt around my brand-spanking-new living space. At least I hadn't moved any furniture in yet, so I could do a deep clean after everyone left.

"You've done a fantastic job," one of the elderly women who came into the store to flirt with Stewie said. "So, do you think you'll be selling it?"

"No, why would I sell it?"

"Well, that's what young Xander Petterson did," said a woman I barely knew, except that she was a notorious town gossip. She was alluding to Xander's success as a house flipper.

"That's interesting. No, I'm not selling."

"I heard he sold the house he inherited from his uncle for three times what he had in it," Stewie said. Then he winked at me.

"That's cool. Canapé?" I pushed the food onto the old people around me.

"Isn't your dad in construction?" Councilman Max asked.

"He is. I worked for him for a time. I'm not one to move around, so this is going to be my forever home."

"There's no shame in moving around," my old high school teacher said as she stepped into the conversation. "Your aunt was an odd one when it came to such things. She held on to this property like it was a lifeline."

"Excuse me." I put the canapé tray down and walked up the stairs to give myself a break.

"That woman is such a troublemaker." I heard the voice behind me and almost moaned before I caught myself. I turned to see Ellen Petterson, Xander's mom.

"You don't have to compare yourself to Xander. He loves the game. I suspect your father does as well. But your aunt Helen, she loved things settled. I'm guessing you're like her."

I smiled and nodded. "I'm not interested in selling my home. I… well, this was what I wanted to do for Aunt Helen. For me too," I quickly added.

"You've done a beautiful job. Helen, bless her, fought this old house her entire life. It needed so much work. I was surprised you didn't just tear it down. The fact that you didn't tells me a lot about you."

She smiled and winked. "So, my poor Xander got called away, chasing that dream of his. You know he's been buried chin-deep in work since… well, for a while."

Clearly she'd caught wind that he'd asked me out, and she was making excuses for him.

"I hope he isn't too buried," I said.

"Come show me the back. I saw you added on a little balcony that leads off the master. I think that's so romantic," she said as she all but pulled me onto the balcony that looked out over the river.

She pointed at the house on the other side. "Xander's been staying there off and on for a while. Poor old house needs a ton of work. Now that you're done with this one, I bet you could give him some pointers."

I chuckled. "You're playing matchmaker, aren't you?"

She laughed out loud. "I thought I was more subtle than that." She slapped my hand. "Xander's a good boy, and I think you are too. Is it horrible that a mother would like to see her son happy?"

I shook my head. "No, my mom's in my social life more than I am. I think it's just part of being a mom."

She laughed again. "I think you might be right. Well, I won't pester you, but I do think the two of you have a lot in common. Come on, I'll help you drive all these folks out of your house so you can get a moment's peace."

"Really? How?" I asked.

"Oh," she said, "watch the expert."

I followed her downstairs, and when she got to the bottom step, she clapped her hands. "Okay, everyone, we've pestered Mr. Healy enough. I talked to Peggy at the café, and she baked pie for us. Said she'd sell it for two dollars a slice."

That seemed to be what they needed to hear. Everyone said bye as they left, and I closed the door, thankful Xander's mom was here to save me. Then I grabbed my broom and cleaned up, determined to get things spotless again so I could start filling my home with furniture tomorrow.

I'd worked more hours at the hardware store than I intended, but Stewie's health was still an issue. So, with my very limited weekend, I was determined to get moved in. The party was a nuisance, but a necessary one. The people of Wilcox needed to see me and know me. A party was a great way to deal with everyone's curiosity without a constant stream of visitors.

As soon as I got everything as clean as I wanted, I locked the house and headed home. I spent an hour planning all the furniture stores I needed to visit tomorrow. I'd rented a U-Haul, and I had two days to find, buy, and bring all my furniture home. Yes, it was a ton of driving, and no, I didn't mind. I wanted to make my house a home.

Next weekend, Mom and Dad and their families were coming, and I wanted everyone's rooms set up—especially the twins. My half sisters needed to know the place as theirs. Just like I'd known it was mine when Aunt Helen lived here. At least now I knew the roof wouldn't fall in on them while they slept—a luxury I never had when I stayed here as a kid.

Xander

"MOM, ARE you here?" I yelled.

When there was no answer, I kicked off my shoes and headed into the kitchen and to the refrigerator.

I smiled when I spotted the sliced ham Mom had put out for me. I had committed to eating less takeout after my belly began to grow and my muscles faded. Eating better and getting exercise had to be a priority when I was on the road as much as I was.

I made a sandwich with her whole wheat bread—which she kept just for me—and sat down at the island to dig in. Mom was going to a party and wanted me to go with her, but I couldn't get home sooner. I'd also rather have my teeth pulled than go to a party after the hellish week I'd had. I was counting the days before this crazy running was over.

When I finished my sandwich, I lay down on the sofa and passed out the moment my head touched the cushion. I heard Mom come back, and when she threw the light on, I slowly sat up, scaring her.

"Xander, child, why did you not say something?" she asked, holding her chest.

"Um, I just woke up? Sorry, Mom." I said.

"Did you eat? Want me to fix you something?" she asked as she hung her jacket on the entry hall tree.

"No, I ate, but I wanted to see you before I headed home. I didn't expect to fall asleep, though."

Mom kissed my head and headed into the kitchen. "You're working too much," she chastised, which wasn't anything new. When she returned, she sat on the chair across from me and sighed. "I came from Rhys Healy's home. He just got it done, and it's truly remarkable what he did with that rat trap. You should've been with me. A man like Rhys doesn't last long, Xander. A smart young man will grab him up, and your chance of wooing him will be gone before you know it."

I chuckled. "Wooing? Mom, I'm not wooing anyone."

"And that's my point, son, you can't spend your life working. You need a partner, someone who can help you navigate life. Someone who makes it nicer to live."

"Mom, I'm happy being single. I don't need a man to make life better."

She shook her head. "I'm not saying you *need* a man. I'm just saying they can make life… better."

I shrugged, then nodded. "I have been thinking about asking him out. Well, I sorta did, but then I got called out of town."

"And," she said, standing up, which was her way of dismissing me, "that's exactly what I told him. Now you need to do the rest yourself, and I recommend you get to it soon."

She kissed me again and then kicked me out. I got into my truck and was headed back to my side of town when I noticed the lights were on in Rhys's place.

I parked the truck in my driveway and walked over the bridge just as Rhys came out. "Hey," I said, causing him to jump. It was the second time tonight I'd startled someone.

"Oh, hey," Rhys said.

"I-I just came from Mom's. She said you were finished and about to move in. I've got some time off. Can you use a couple of extra hands?" I smiled at his eager look.

"Really?" he asked.

I nodded. "Yep, really."

"Yeah, I'm going up to Eugene, and I have to buy furniture and move it here, and I only have tomorrow and Sunday to get it all done."

"Then my hands and my truck are all yours," I said.

"Oh man, that's so generous."

When he gave me a time, I waved and headed back to my place. It was a much earlier start time than I would've liked, considering all I'd just finished dealing with, but if it meant a few extra hours with him, I'd be happy.

I wanted to kiss him, but I decided to scurry back to my side of the bridge. If I were lucky, after a day of helping out, he'd be more willing to let me have that kiss, and if I were really lucky, I'd have the energy to do a lot more. As exhausted as I was, and with my nap cut short, I was ready for real sleep.

When I returned to the ugly house, I cringed. I vowed that it would be the next project, even if I had to live with Mom. She'd hate that, but damn, it was long past time for the monstrosity to go away. I wanted to finish the house plans and start construction.

I needed to restore the historic houses in this part of town if I was ever going to get Wilcox on board with my ultimate goal to develop the town's commercial elements.

I plopped into bed, and despite the fatigue, I thought of how sexy Rhys had looked. When I startled him, it was everything I had in me not to pull him into my arms and tease him. I was looking forward to tomorrow. I was really, really looking forward to tomorrow.

Rhys

"You know, I didn't mean to blow you off. I got called in to work," Xander said as we drove toward Eugene.

"Yeah, thanks, your mom told me."

I nodded and smiled. "So, how was it having all the town up in your business?" he asked, and I couldn't help but moan.

"Couldn't be helped," I responded with a sigh. "I love this little town, but folks want to be *all* in your business. Oh, and they kept asking me if I was selling. Like, for real, they thought because *you* buy and sell homes, naturally, I should."

He glanced at me, bewildered. "Your dad flips houses, doesn't he?"

I groaned again. "Yeah, and I'm not my dad." I stared out the window and tried not to get frustrated again.

When I finally glanced back, he smiled at me. "I didn't mean to insinuate you were. Just, you know, folks are sorta used to people coming into town, doing stuff, and disappearing again. There's not many people our age settling in Wilcox these days."

I nodded. "I think that might change eventually. Wilcox is on the interstate and not that far from Eugene, but I'm not really interested in flipping. I, well, I'm like my aunt. I want a place where I can stick. That probably doesn't make much sense to you." He laughed, and I looked over, shocked. "What?"

"I'm trying to figure out how to stick too. Just so you know, I'm about to build several homes on the other side of the river from you. I bought the ugly modern house over there and am going to have it torn down and put more appropriate homes back up."

That shocked me. The monstrosity he was talking about was an eyesore, but I could only imagine that it'd be worth a pretty penny when it was fixed up. "So, what kind of houses?" I asked.

"Well, not much different from yours. Something that reflects the architecture over there, so think 1920s."

"Really?" I didn't know how to react to that. It wasn't the kind of thing someone would do if they wanted to make fast money and run. Maybe he *was* thinking about sticking.

"Well, if you need a contractor, my dad would love it. Or are you going to do it yourself?" I asked.

"No, I don't have time. But yeah, I'd like to talk to your dad or… well, what about you?"

"Me?" I asked. "I'm more of a grunt worker, not someone you'd hire to do the management."

He laughed. "Listen, I watched you turn your aunt's house from a sty into something anyone would be proud to live in—no offense to your aunt. I also watched you deal with all the subs, and honestly, you're good. Respectful, sympathetic. I even saw when your roofing guy broke down and yelled at you. You handled that like a pro."

I forced my mouth shut as I stared at him. "You were watching me?"

"Hard not to when I live right across the river. But don't get too upset. I wasn't here enough to do much snooping, just enough to see you're good at it."

I leaned back against the seat. "My dad harassed me for years to take over project management. I resisted, but I did enjoy it. I'm not promising anything, 'cause I might hate it, but if you do hire my father, and he wants me to take on the management, I'll consider it. For now, let's talk about your design skills."

I wanted to change the subject. I would like to do the project, if only to ensure I had some control over what was happening in my community. I just wasn't ready to commit to it yet.

Xander and I exchanged ideas. I was pleasantly surprised to learn he was pretty good at design. I could figure out how to maximize a living space and honor all the historical elements while making it modern and usable. But what cushion color wasn't my forte.

I had shown the house to Xander, and he came up with some great ideas for how to decorate without making me feel like I'd filled the space with boring garbage when I'd just worked so hard to put it right.

We stopped in several big-box stores and found a comfortable but reserved sofa and recliner for upstairs, and the sectional I wanted for my basement mancave. Those were easy, since I'd already picked them out online. The rest required a lot more patience, and I knew I'd have given up long before we bought the last pillow had Xander not been with me.

"Okay, come on. My favorite hole-in-the-wall bar is just over here." I pointed toward a little building just off the main stretch. I laughed when I caught Xander's expression as we got out of the car. "Come on. It's much better than it looks."

"Can't be worse without being condemned," he said, making me laugh again.

"Just remember, most of their business is at night, long after dark. This is a big university hangout."

"Is that how you learned about the place?" he asked.

"No, I didn't go to school here. I went to a community college in Salem. Then I figured out I preferred electricity over books."

Xander smiled. "I managed to get through college, then realized basically the same thing, just a lot of student loans too late."

"Ugh, yeah, I know about those. Luckily, I don't have any, since the community college was cheap and Dad covered my electrician studies. He had a vested interest, after all."

We went into the bar and, with Xander's permission, ordered the best hamburgers in Oregon. They delivered them as we talked shop, and Xander stared at his. "That's a huge burger," he said.

"Yeah, if I'd known you better, I'd have talked you into sharing one. That's what Dad and I do when we come here."

"You should've anyway," he said, but he picked up the burger. I watched him smile. If he liked food, he was in for a treat, and I wanted to watch.

He bit into it, and when the flavors hit him, his eyes flew open, and then he closed them and moaned with delight. I know it's sorta stupid and maybe a bit cliché, but watching him experience the ecstasy of the burger caused all my sexual cylinders to fire.

Xander was taller than me, and his neck was taut with muscles that contracted in the fucking sexiest way as he chewed and swallowed. "My God," he said, drawing my attention back to his eyes, "that's amazing."

I swallowed hard and forced my thoughts away from licking those neck muscles. "Yeah," I squeaked, "it's the best in Oregon."

When I looked into his eyes, he stopped chewing and stared at me. Clearly, I hadn't hidden my attraction. "You know, we can take this to go," he whispered, and a chill ran through me.

I shook my head. "No, it's a long way back to Wilcox, and… well, something tells me we should take things slow. Not that I want to, but we're neighbors, and sex complicates things."

Xander winked when I stopped blabbing. "Yeah, but sometimes life is better when it's complicated."

I didn't have a response, so I picked up my own burger and took a bite. Juicy deliciousness burst over my tongue, and I didn't even try to force down the thought of what else might taste amazing.

Xander

OKAY, RHYS was cute—even more so now I'd gotten to know him. He was reserved, and I'd known that before, but once I got him to come out of his shell, I found him funny too. He liked a lot of the same things I did.

He let me lead him around the big-box stores to buy decorations for his home. Which, by the way, was magnificent. He'd used a lot of light wood on the walls and trim—nothing dark, but nothing so light it looked like it was from the 1990s either. Thank God. Living in my '90s monstrosity, it would've turned me off.

I instinctively knew he'd need some color that accented the beautiful architecture. It was fun teasing him as he gravitated toward muted colors. But when I found a maple box and put the dark against it, then showed him a bright blue color, he could see why bold colors were the better choice.

By the time we went to eat, I thought he wasn't that into me, since he hadn't made any kind of move. But I was pretty sure he and I made a good team. I'd already broached the subject of him managing the construction of the new homes on my side of the river. I had already decided to ask, mostly because I knew the town would have seen his work on his house and would respect him. But I meant to wait to discuss it. So much for my ability to keep my thoughts to myself.

After our sexual eye exchange, I'd have been willing to rent a hotel room, but he quashed the idea, saying getting involved would be complicated.

Yeah, I thought, things were definitely going to get complicated, because I wanted him more than ever, and now I knew he felt the same. It would happen one way or another, even if I did have to wait.

Mom had said I needed to woo the man, and maybe she was right, not that she wasn't usually, but yeah, I was totally about to start wooing Rhys Healy. The sooner I had that tight little body under me, the better.

I kept the conversation light as I drove us back to Wilcox. The ground was dry enough for me to back the truck up to his house, but barely, and I helped him unload and set the furniture. The damned bedroom furniture he bought wasn't going to be delivered until tomorrow, so that threw a bit of a wrench in the wooing plans. Well, okay, *sexing* plans.

We set up his living room and stored the dishes in his kitchen. Then we went to his rental home and collected the rest of his belongings. Luckily, that included beer, which, after he'd put everything away, he invited me to sit and enjoy with him.

To my happy surprise, Rhys sat right next to me on his new sofa. I didn't even take a sip of the beer. Instead, I put it on the coaster on the coffee table and turned to him.

He smiled and closed the gap between us. He tasted of summer. His skin was soft and moist from the work we'd done unloading. I wanted so much of this man. It was all I could do not to jump him.

When he pulled back, I groaned. "You... you're so hot, Rhys. I really do want you."

"Same," he whispered so softly I almost didn't hear him. "You sure, though? I mean—"

I didn't let him finish. Luckily, he'd put his beer down, because I pushed his body onto his new sofa and assaulted his mouth, devouring him, taking all he was willing to give.

I forced myself to go slow. The first time, I wanted it to be about Rhys. I probably should've let him take the reins too, but when he didn't insist, I took the lead.

Rhys stared into my eyes as I pulled his shirt up over his head and tasted his delicious neck. His sweet moans prompted me to go further, to give him more.

I sucked on his neck, careful not to leave a hickey—no need to get the town going over that. But oh, I so could've if I weren't forcing myself to go easy—something that was becoming more difficult the fewer clothes he had on.

When I got his pants off, it was my turn to moan. His cock was beautiful and stood at attention, asking to be sucked. I didn't hesitate. I took him into my mouth and played with his head, building upon the natural sensitivity and waiting to hear proof I was doing what he enjoyed.

When the sounds of pleasure escaped him, I bore down and took his entire length into my mouth. He instantly bucked against me and shoved his long cock even farther down my throat.

I didn't resist when he began to fuck my mouth, and I could tell he was close to climax. I was ready to taste the salty come, but he stopped and forced me back. "My turn," he said, and I looked up at his flushed but happy face.

I nodded, stripped off the rest of my clothes, and sat in the place he'd just vacated. Rhys knelt between my legs and took my girth into his hand. He looked up at me, and those sexy eyes of his, staring at me in this seductive way, were enough to make me come just sitting there.

He leaned over and, without taking his eyes from mine, swiped his tongue across my slit. For just a moment, I saw my precum sitting on the tip of his tongue. Then he drew it in and swallowed, clearly enjoying the taste of me. Fuck, I liked that and couldn't wait to see my seed spilled on that pretty face of his.

I was savoring that thought when Rhys sucked me back into his throat and swallowed. "Fuck," I growled as all my nerve endings caught fire.

I kept repeating it as that hot, expert mouth glided up and down my shaft, taking me to the brink, then pulling back. Time and again, he edged me, and each time those mischievous eyes returned to mine, he waited just long enough that I was all but whimpering with need before he sucked me back into his mouth again.

It was too much, too fucking much, and when he edged me again, it was more than I could handle. I got up when he pulled back, stood, and brought his mouth back up to my head. "Take my cock," I demanded, and Rhys didn't disappoint.

I forced myself not to batter his mouth, but Rhys clearly had other ideas. He grabbed my ass and, pulling me forward, took my cock again. That's all the permission I needed. "Take it," I demanded, and holding his head, I fucked his throat, taking all the pleasure he was willing to give.

I felt my orgasm building, and fuck if I wasn't going to have my way this time. I took my cock out of his mouth just as the orgasm hit me, and I leaned back in ecstasy as I came all over that gorgeous face. I looked down and swallowed hard, seeing my seed on him. I was kinky as fuck. I knew that about myself, but not all guys are. I didn't want to chase him away, but when his tongue slipped out to lap up the cum that dripped down his lips, that was all the invitation I needed.

I kissed him, tasting myself, then licked my cum and kissed him again. Fuck if he didn't enjoy it. God, this man was so perfect for me.

I literally stood him up then, and face fucked myself with his cock, desperate to return the same passion he'd gifted me. It didn't take long before his body went rigid and his seed poured into my mouth.

Rhys bent down and kissed me, basically snowballing, "Kinky little fucker," I said.

"You have no idea," he whispered, and fuck if that didn't wake my sleeping cock back up.

Breathless, I replied, "I can't wait to find out.

Rhys

I WANTED TO feel guilty. I mean, I should feel, maybe not guilty, but regretful. I had just had a mind-blowing blowjob with a mind-blowing man, and he was my fucking neighbor. I should be concerned. However, the only thing I kept thinking was, *When can we do it again?*

I'd filled the hot tub the day before, so it was nice and warm, and with a pause in the rain, I tugged Xander out the basement door and into the tub. He let me kiss him as the jets massaged us. God, if I'd known the first time I used the tub would be with a man as sexy as Xander, I'd have filled it the day I finished installing it.

When I finally lay back next to him and let the jets pound my back, Xander snuggled close. "Mmm, you feel good," I admitted to his chuckle.

"Same," he replied, and we sat like that until the jets turned off. "I should probably get home. I have to work tomorrow."

I looked at him and searched to see if this was a one-night thing. As he stood, he pulled me up with him and kissed me again. "I'm sure I'll be pulled out of town again, but I've already taken Friday off. I'm meeting an architect to go over my plans for the houses. Wanna join me?" he asked.

I considered it, then crawled out of the tub and toweled off. "Xander, is it smart to be involved like this?" I said, waving my hand between us. "And doing business together?"

He shrugged. "Business with benefits works for me," he replied.

"You're a mess. Okay, why not? If you want, I'll let Dad know you're looking to hire someone for the project. Once I see your plans, I can fill him in on the work."

Xander winked as he pulled me into the basement and out of the cool night air. "Want to shower with me before I go?" he asked.

I did, but thinking maybe he wanted to go, I hadn't asked. "Yeah." I nodded and wished it hadn't sounded shy. I wasn't great at the dating game. My emotions were too obviously on my sleeve. Isn't that how the saying goes?

I liked sex. I liked sex more when a guy took the reins. I don't know why. I liked a man who knew how to get what he wanted without me having to be responsible. Of course, I had needs too. "I don't have a condom, I'm on PrEP, and I'm clean. Just got tested, even." I said.

"Yeah, same, PrEP, but haven't had sex in a while, so if I had something else, I'd know. So, can we?" Xander asked. His expression was like a kid asking for a forbidden piece of candy.

I nodded, happy we'd moved my stuff over so I knew exactly where my lube was. I lathered up his big, sexy body, christening my two-person basement shower, and took the time to enjoy what Xander's very tight body felt like under my hands.

He let me have my way this time, which honestly felt nice. When he got his hands full of soap and washed me down, he spent a good amount of time rubbing our lathered cocks together, each of us rutting into the pleasure.

Then he turned me around and lined that soaped-up cock up to my ass and jacked me off as his cock teased my hole.

"Fuck, I-I want you inside me," I finally whimpered, no longer caring what that sounded like. I was so fucking horny. I needed him.

He gave that deep dark chuckle of his, which sent shivers through me. Then he reached up, took the lube, and poured it over my ass and his cock.

He teased me a little more and pulled more moans of need and desire out of me. It'd been a while since I'd had anal sex. Fuck, it'd been a while since I'd had *any* sex. So I figured it would take some prep, but fuck, the moment the head of his cock hit my hole, I knew all I wanted was that inside me.

He took his time as he slowly let the head stretch me. "Fuck, fuck yeah," I screamed, and thanked all that was good that he knew how to use that tool.

He massaged my neck and shoulders as his cock slowly pushed deeper. "Yes," I yelled. Then, when he was far enough in, the stinging stopped and the intense pleasure of having a man as big as Xander inside me took over. I moved as he pulled out and then pushed back, fucking myself with his cock.

Two, three, four times, and that was it, my brain was scrambled. "Fuck... fuck me, Xander," I demanded.

He didn't hesitate. He reached down and held the front of my hip with his right hand while the other rested on the wall above us. Using his right to control us, he fucked into me. "God damn, fuck… yes, all of it," I demanded again and again.

I wanted it all. I wanted everything Xander had to give, so I instinctively knew to put my hands against the new tile and arch my back, causing Xander's pounding to deepen. "Fucking… fuck!" I moaned as his cock hit my prostate again and again.

I forced myself to let go of my cock, not wanting the intensity to end. Then he moved, and this time, when his cock hit my prostate full-on, I came all over the tiles. "Aaah," I heard behind me as his orgasm hit him and he emptied inside my ass.

I didn't usually let guys fuck me bare. I, well, shit, I wanted all this man could give me, and in that moment, knowing his seed was being thrust deep inside me felt… right. How the fuck did I explain that?

He held me for a long time until the water began to cool. Then we quickly washed the lube and cum away, turned off the water, and dried off.

After he dressed, I kissed him good night and felt slightly disappointed he didn't want to spend the night. Maybe if I were lucky, there'd be more opportunities.

I was restless after he left, and felt as if I'd missed something because I didn't get the afterglow cuddle I usually never wanted with a man. I wandered around my new space, amazed at how beautiful the furniture was with the accessories Xander had convinced me to purchase. Somehow, he'd perfectly reflected my style in a way I couldn't.

I ended up sleeping downstairs on the sofa we'd already christened. The basement hadn't been usable at all when my aunt lived here, but damn, I was so happy I'd spent the extra to have it built. I knew without a shadow of a doubt, now especially, that this would easily be one of my favorite places in the house.

THE NEXT morning I woke to my father's frantic phone call. "Rhys, can you come to Portland? Your stepmom is sick, and I need someone to take care of the girls."

I gripped my phone and sat up. "Dad, what's wrong?"

"Lucy had a miscarriage, an ectopic pregnancy, they said. Her fallopian tube ruptured. I don't know all the details, but she's in the ICU. I'm at the hospital with the girls. Her mom's coming in, but—"

"Dad, don't worry, I'll be there. Tell Lucy I'm thinking of her. Give me a few hours, and I'll pick up the girls and take them home."

I heard someone I assumed was the nurse talking to Dad before he hung up. Shit, well, at least they caught it. I didn't know much about all that, but if she was in the ICU, it must be serious. I grabbed a shower, locked up, and rushed to the hospital.

I glanced at the little rental and sighed. I'd told my landlord buddy I'd have all my stuff out this week. I had most of it out, but I'd have to pay extra. But I let all that go as I rushed to Portland to be with my family.

The girls grabbed me into a hug the moment I walked in. "Rhys, Mom is sick," Chelsie said.

"I know, honey, but I think she's going to be okay."

Jenny, by far the more reserved of the two, hung close by, and when Chelsie let go, I hugged her as well. Then I kissed their temples like always. Dad embraced me as soon as I stood up. "How's Lucy?" I asked.

He nodded. "She's sad but fine. They moved her to a regular room and are going to monitor her to make sure there's no more bleeding."

I nodded. "Can I go and say hi?"

Dad nodded, and I told him I'd only be a moment, then I'd take the girls home.

Lucy was crying when I entered, and I sat beside her and took her hand. "Hi, Luce," I said.

"Hey, sorry you had to come all this way."

"Nonsense, you knew I'd come. Can I get you anything?" I asked, and she just shook her head.

I had looked ectopic pregnancies up on the way and knew she'd probably lost her tube. Lucy had cancer before marrying Dad, and they'd removed the other one. As a stepson, I doubted I could give her much support. But I could make sure she and Dad had enough time to work through the pain together.

"I'm going to take the girls home. Dad said they wanted to go to school, so I'm going to make sure that's done, okay?"

She just nodded and closed her eyes, and I squeezed her hand. I wish I could've offered more support, but Lucy's mom was one of those women full of love, and I guessed she would be better at comforting her than I could.

Dad hugged me again before we left, and I installed the girls' car seats in the back of my truck.

Kids are interesting… and pretty strong. Despite all the drama with their mom, they talked about school and some boy they thought was cute. Lucy wasn't even my mom, and my heart felt like it'd been stomped on.

We ended up not getting the girls to school that day. By the time they got home and ate, there were only a couple of hours left. So, since the school had me listed as one of the girls' caregivers, I called and told them Lucy was in the hospital, but the girls would be back to school tomorrow.

We watched reruns of *The Mandalorian* on Disney for most of the day. Jenny had a bit of a crush on Pedro Pascal as Mando. Of course, the three posters of him on her wall would clue anyone in.

I'd kept the girls so many times over the years, it was natural for me. I usually would've made them do homework or chores, but with Lucy in the hospital, I figured TV was the best way to get through our day.

I fixed their favorite mac-n-cheese with chicken nuggets and the dreaded steamed broccoli their mom insisted on. They ate without fuss, and I sent them up to bathe and get ready for bed. They had questions about Lucy and wanted to know about the baby she'd lost.

I didn't even know Dad had mentioned that to them, but they were smarter than the average bear. If they heard pregnancy, they knew what it meant.

I was holding the book Dad usually read to them at night, but I didn't open it. Instead, I drew a deep breath to gather my thoughts. "So, the baby wasn't really a baby. It was trying to be, but it got stuck, and well, long story short, your mom isn't going to have one."

Chelsie looked at Jenny and said, "I told you, she can't have no more babies."

I cocked my eyebrow and decided to let Dad and Lucy know they'd have to figure out how to handle the conversation later. "So, I'm going to read a little now, unless you're tired."

Both girls nodded, so I found the place in the story and read until they looked about to fall asleep. I closed the book and kissed my little sisters on their foreheads and then dimmed the light and cracked the door.

My room was down the hall, over the garage. I'd lived in the apartment while I worked for Dad. It was technically self-contained, which is what made it viable for me to live in, but there was a door to the main house from the living room. The girls knew they could get me if they needed anything.

I called Dad to check on Lucy and was told they were going to keep her a little longer, which I thought was strange, but I put it out of my head and assured him I'd get the girls to school tomorrow.

That night I lay in bed staring at the ceiling, thinking about the day. It had been intense. I hadn't second-guessed my decision to move to Wilcox until now. Dad, Mom, Lucy, and the girls—they were my family, and they were all here in Portland while I was so far away.

My thoughts drifted to Aunt Helen. Wilcox was our legacy, and it felt like that for me. I didn't want to give that up to live in Portland, but I didn't want to leave my family either. I closed my eyes on the dilemma, and images of Xander immediately came to mind, making me smile.

He'd felt so amazing as we made love. Yeah, I was a ridiculous romantic to call it that, especially as deliciously naughty as both bouts of sex had been, but I liked him more than just as a quick fuck—not like the guy I'd met a few months back in Eugene. He'd been sexy, hot, and buff, but once the excitement was over, I was ready for him to go.

I'd pretty much felt that way about every man until now. Why did I want Xander to come back for a second performance? I had no idea, but it didn't matter, not really. I still didn't think I was Xander Petterson's type. Ultimately I doubted there'd be a relationship there, just a nice distraction while I was in Wilcox.

I cringed as I had that thought, *while I was in Wilcox*. Did that mean I might not be staying? Ugh, I couldn't decide right then. I certainly didn't want to leave it, but how could I not be close to my family? Especially when things like this could happen?

I closed my eyes and forced the thoughts out of my mind. I couldn't solve anything now, regardless. I just had to take things as they came.

Xander

I HAD A great relationship with my bosses—at least that's what I thought. They had a hundred and one projects going on all the freaking time, and I managed over half of them. It wasn't like me to complain about work. I was raised by an old farmer who repeatedly reminded me he'd had to get up to milk cows in the morning before school.

Luckily, he hadn't stayed a farmer, but those values had been fiercely ingrained into me. I didn't mind work and didn't complain about it, but with my Wilcox projects, I had expected them to let up a bit now that I needed some time.

I couldn't have been more wrong. I showed up at the office in Salem Monday morning and had just begun to put out the fires from the weekend when my boss came in and told me I was needed Friday.

"Nope, can't do it. Got plans."

"Not negotiable," he said, and he walked out.

What the fuck? I thought. *Not negotiable.*

I took a few moments to get my temper under control, and then I went to his office, knocked, and walked in. "Leon, I asked for Friday off months ago. I have—"

"I said it was nonnegotiable, Xander. Now that's the end of it."

"May I remind you I have over three months of comp time I'm owed, and that I'm owed that because I haven't taken a day off since I've been here?"

Leon looked up at me and squinted. "Are you threatening me?" he asked.

I paused momentarily, then nodded. "Yeah, I think if you're going to treat me like this, then I may no longer belong with this company," I said. Then I walked out.

I had quite a lot of money put away since I basically didn't have a social life and hadn't since I started working here. That didn't mean I was ready to be unemployed. I fully intended to use my leverage with the company to get the work I dreamed of doing in Wilcox.

I sat down at my desk, then groaned when Leon came in behind me, pointed his finger in my face, and began to yell. Leon was a hothead. I knew that, had known it since I started here. But I hadn't faced his temper. I hadn't had to, because I was always willing to do whatever was required.

"If you can't do the fucking job, you can get the fuck out," he yelled, and something snapped. I had worked here all these years with no complaints and no drama, giving every free hour to the company, and this was what I got?

I pulled a box out of the corner from an Amazon delivery I'd had last week and began to pack up my desk. "What the fuck are you doing? "Leon yelled.

"Getting the fuck out of here," I said calmly.

I think Leon was surprised. When he went toe to toe with someone, he never backed down, but I didn't look up to see why he was quiet. I was done. I'd have my attorney contact the company to figure out how to deal with the months of comp time they owed me.

I expected the owner's son, James Hendrix, to show up at any moment to talk me off the ledge, and I knew that my assistant would already have told him there was drama going down. Yet I left the office that day with my box of personal items in my hand and no one tried to stop me.

My heart beat wildly as I put the box in the back of the truck and shut the door. "What the hell just happened?" I asked myself. Was it possible I'd just left a job that'd been my life for so long?

I shook my head, let out the deep breath I'd been holding, and started the truck. I was almost back to Wilcox when I decided to call my attorney and have them contact the company to figure out the details. Regardless of how things went, they at least owed me the time I hadn't taken.

I'd had enough insight to get funding for the new homes I hoped to build in Wilcox. Thankfully, they'd taken my bank account as leverage, not my job, so I didn't have to worry about losing the project. I just had to finish the architectural drawings and get the town council's approval. Not an easy feat, considering that just last year I'd been in trouble with the county for illegally painting two covered bridges.

By the time I got back to Wilcox, I was feeling damned good. For years my work had kept me from doing what I wanted. It had taken over my entire life. I knew I would eventually quit, but I'd held on because of the security working there had given me. Now I was free to do what I wanted.

I parked the truck in the driveway of my ugly house and rushed over the bridge to Rhys's place, hoping to tell him what had happened. Unfortunately he didn't answer my knock, and his truck wasn't in the driveway. I just wanted a congratulatory fuck, but maybe I could get that later. For now, I wanted to see if I could get this building project ratcheted up.

I glanced across the street and saw the little rental that Rhys had been living in. I knew it would be perfect for me while the project I was about to start was underway. It seemed like things were working out. Now, if I could get the sexy Rhys to agree to help me, we could get these houses built faster.

Rhys

THE BOTTOM fell out from under me as my father sat across the dining table, tears streaming down his face. "The cancer's returned. They only found it because of the miscarriage."

I sat dumbfounded, not sure what to say. "Um, what're they going to do?" I asked.

He shook his head. "It's spread, but… they think they can treat it—some experimental therapy."

I listened as he talked about the cancer center they'd have to go to for the treatment. "Rhys, we need you to take care of the girls."

I nodded. "Of course, Dad."

We sat silently and let everything he'd said settle between us. Lucy was in real danger right now. Then there were the girls. So much to consider.

"So, how long will the treatment last?" I asked as I considered what that would mean to my life. Stewie still hadn't fully recovered, and I would need to get back to work. Not to mention… well, Xander probably shouldn't be a consideration.

"Months. I'm sorry, but we need you."

I nodded. "Dad," I said, suddenly decisive, "you and I both have to go home to Wilcox. It only makes sense for the girls to as well. I'm going to take them back with me. You know the schools are as good as the private one you're paying for here. Besides, we're closer to California than you are here. If you've got to travel to the cancer center by car, then—"

Dad sighed. "I was hoping you'd take over here." He shook his head. "I guess I knew you wouldn't. The girls will enjoy Wilcox. I'll talk to Lucy."

I reached over, took his hand in mine, and squeezed. "Listen, focus on making Lucy better, okay? My sisters and I will be just fine."

He smiled and nodded. "Okay," he said, then he repeated it, and I heard the resolution in his voice. "Okay."

THE GIRLS were able to spend a few days with their mom before she flew to the cancer center in California. They were confused, as I figured they would be, but Lucy was great telling them the truth, but not in a scary way.

"You'll be staying with Rhys in Wilcox while we—your daddy and I and your grandma Joan—will fix all my sore spots."

Joan lived in Texas in a senior living complex. She'd had a stroke a few years back, which stopped her from being able to take care of the girls, but I was glad she was going to be with Lucy. Dad was a good man but wasn't the best with his emotions. Hell, I guess I'm not that great either.

Luckily there were several guys Dad could rely on at work, so he didn't push me to come back. We talked with the school in Wilcox and got all the girls' paperwork transferred. Then I drove us back the day after Lucy and Dad went to begin her treatment.

It'd been a long-ass week. My nerves were frayed, as were the girls'. The school wanted them to come to class on Friday to meet the teacher and the other kids so they'd still have the weekend off before they started on Monday.

When I got a text from Xander wanting to hang out, I told him what had happened, and he offered his condolences. It put the brakes on our… whatever we were. I hadn't expected to see him again, and now I had my six-year-old sisters to take care of, but he called Friday morning asking if I could still meet the architect.

I needed to get to the hardware store and make sure Stewie was okay, but I could do that and still meet him, so I agreed, although I wasn't sure what he expected. I certainly couldn't imagine taking on anything else right now.

Stewie was happy to see me, and by the look of the store, I could understand why. I dropped the girls at the school and then spent the morning restocking and cleaning up the mess. I wanted to tell him he needed to consider hiring someone else, but with the vulnerability I saw in his expression, I didn't have it in me. Not yet, anyway.

I was able to get away by eleven with plenty of time to meet Xander and his architect in one of the few downtown shops still being used as a business. Xander surprised me when he kissed me in front of the old man we were meeting. But when I pulled back, the old guy was smiling.

Ugh, I knew from my experience at the hardware store that this would be front-and-center gossip now. Oh well, the kiss was one of the highlights of my week, even if it was chaste. It felt good that he was happy to see me and wasn't afraid to kiss me in front of the townsfolk.

For the next hour, I watched as the ancient man who had already announced he would be ninety next year showed us the plans for the six houses to be built on Xander's property on that side of the river. They were beautiful, and each reflected the older style Xander said he was going for.

All the houses had real porches, which surprised me. Even the communities in Portland that used older styles had only put in "porchlets." These were valid infill houses that would complement and improve the properties on that side of the bridge.

By the time we were done, I was excited—more than I thought possible. "Hey, do you have time for a beer before you have to pick your sisters up?" Xander asked, and I was weirdly touched by the fact that he had taken my new schedule and responsibilities into account.

"Um, yeah," I said as I looked at my watch. "I have to be there by three."

Xander rolled up the plans, and we shook the old architect's hand as he left. "So, what do you think?" Xander asked as soon as we were seated in the little bar.

"I think it's awesome. Those are going to be great additions to the neighborhood."

"And are you willing to help me build them? I could use your expertise."

I chuckled. "I doubt that, but thanks for saying so."

Xander sighed. "I'm not just being nice. I quit my job, and I'm going to do this full-time, but I've done commercial for the past few years. You've been building communities with your dad, and I need help."

I sighed. "First, sorry about your job. Was that a good thing?"

Xander smiled. "It was a shock, but yeah, it's a good thing."

I nodded. "Well, I have a lot on my plate right now—my stepmom's cancer, my sisters, and I'm also committed to Stewie. The truth is, I'm worried about him."

Xander nodded solemnly. "Do you think he's going to be forced to sell?" he asked.

I lowered my voice so the eavesdroppers couldn't listen. "I don't know how he can avoid it. The store was in bad shape, and I was only gone a few days."

Xander looked concerned, but there were too many listening ears—if we didn't want Stewie to get word of us speaking about him, that is.

"Think about it. I still have to get approval from the city council, then I've got to find subs, so it'll be a while before I need someone to take on the work. But yeah, consider it, if you will."

I reached over and took his hand. "Why don't you come by tonight and meet the girls? I think I'm going to get pizza."

Xander shook his head, then paused and smiled. "I have a better idea. Mom is cooking dinner tonight. She always cooks like she's feeding an army. Why don't I see if she minds you joining us?"

"No." I quickly put my hand up. "I don't want to overstimulate the girls. They have enough going on. I should keep them home tonight."

Xander nodded, but he was already typing on his phone. Before he looked up, his phone dinged. "Hold on," he said, pushing the Call button.

"Hey, Mom," he said when she answered. "Rhys doesn't want to force the girls out tonight. Can we bring dinner to them?"

I wanted to argue, but at the same time, I wanted to spend time with him. His face lit up, and he looked over at me. "Mom said she has a frozen lasagna, and she'd happily warm that up at your place if you want."

I smiled. "Yeah, that works. I think it'd be good for the girls to meet more people in town, as long as it's not the *whole* town," I said quickly, remembering she had arranged the open-house thing.

Xander nodded a few times and then hung up. "Mom's excited to meet the kids and to cook something in your new fancy kitchen."

I just laughed. "Does she know she'll be the first person to use it?" I asked.

"Oh no, this is going to make her over-the-moon excited. I'll let her know," he said.

When I glanced down at my watch and saw I only had half an hour to get to the school, I stood up. I wanted to talk to the teacher and principal to find out how the day went.

Xander didn't hesitate to kiss me in the bar right in front of the whole town. That took some getting used to, but I also liked it. Did I want to be claimed? I wasn't sure, but I decided I'd just enjoy it as it happened. I'd figure out the details later.

Xander

OKAY, A BIT pushy. I admit. But I couldn't help myself. I'd missed Rhys, and although I knew he wanted to protect his little sisters, I wanted to spend time with him.

A few years back, I dated a guy who had kids, and at first he didn't want his kids to meet me, afraid it'd upset the apple cart. In the end, that's what broke us up. I didn't want that to happen with Rhys, so I figured it was best to get to know the girls right away, provided he would let me.

I also might've had an ulterior motive, inviting Mom. She'd begun to hint heavily at grandchildren. Apparently she'd recently met a local gay couple who had children. Now she'd begun to say things like, "You know, you can have kids even if you aren't married."

I thought I could use Rhys's sisters as her pseudo grandchildren, and that might help take the heat off me for a minute. But then I snickered at my stupidity. My mom would never give up hope, even if she fell head over heels in love with Rhys's sisters.

It was worth a try, at least, right?

I left the bar and headed to the grocery store to grab garlic bread, and when I saw a Baby Yoda coloring book, I grabbed two. Rhys had mentioned the girls were fans. I also found a huge pack of Crayola crayons and thought, *twins... best get two.* I didn't have siblings, but I had cousins, and I hated sharing with them when we were kids. I had to assume the girls were the same.

I pulled up at Rhys's just as he and the girls were going inside. I got out with my arms full, and as I walked in behind them, I was instantly introduced to the twins.

"Hey, Xander, wanna meet my sisters?" he asked, and I quickly put the stuff down and shook their hands.

"Hi, I'm Xander," I said.

"I'm Chelsie," one of the girls said as I shook her hand. "This is my sister, Jenny."

"Why do you always introduce me?" Jenny said, scowling.

"'Cause you're shy. I was trying to help."

The two argued while Rhys shrugged and gently moved his sisters toward the house. "Girls, go take your stuff to your room, but leave your school supply list on the table. I have to…. Ugh, whatever," he said as the two were already up the stairs, having totally ignored him.

I chuckled. "Well, I don't have siblings, but I do have cousins. Looks like you all have a pretty normal relationship."

"You have no idea," Rhys said, but he was smiling. "I'll get it later. When they start arguing, no one else exists, not even their older brother."

"Oh, wait," I said, and I rushed out to get the food and their gifts.

When I returned, I asked what temperature to heat the oven, and Rhys smiled. "You're already bribing my sisters with Mando, I see," he said, and at first, I had no idea what he meant.

"Mandalorian… Baby Yoda." He pointed at the coloring books I'd put on the table.

"Oh, yeah, you said they like them."

Rhys smiled. "You remembered. Cool."

"Yeah," I said, feeling a bit bashful. I'm not sure why, but Rhys made me feel like an awkward teenager.

"So, how long does this need to cook?" he asked, changing the subject.

Rhys put the frozen lasagna into the oven and we chatted while it cooked. It took a good two hours from frozen, and the garlic bread could go in later. When he was done, I slipped behind him and tucked my arms around his waist. "I missed you a lot," I admitted.

Rhys leaned back into my arms as I hoped he would. He all but purred. "I'm glad," he whispered. "But unless you want to explain our relationship, or whatever we have, you best not let my sisters catch you doing this."

I chuckled as I kissed his neck, and he shivered but pulled back— luckily in time to avoid the two girls stampeding back down the stairs. "We're hungry," one of the girls said. I couldn't remember for the life of me which was which. They had different shirt colors, but I hadn't paid attention when they introduced themselves.

"Xander's mom sent over lasagna, and it won't be ready for a while. I can make you peanut butter and jelly, but only half. You two are horrible about eating and losing your appetite before dinner."

"I don't like peanut butter," one of the girls said.

Rhys cocked an eyebrow. "Um, since when?"

"Since just now."

"Whatever. What are you wanting?"

"Ice cream," she said, a naughty smile forming.

"Not happening. I told you, we only eat ice cream before supper when you get an A on your report card. This isn't that kind of day."

"Uh-huh," the other sister said. "We got a new school and already have a friend."

"Oh, and who is this friend?" he asked, fully engrossed in the girl's conversation.

They described a kid who liked to wear frilly clothes. "With ruffles," they said.

I could imagine the kid in my mind. "I don't like dresses," one of the girls said, looking at me. "They make me itch."

Rhys snorted and shook his head. "You don't have to wear dresses, Jenny, but I think I've been convinced about the ice cream. It's been a special day. First let's call your mom, though. I know she's gonna want to know about your first day in school."

The girls' faces dropped, and my heart followed suit. "We don't want her to worry," Chelsie said. I could tell which was which now that Rhys had called one of them Jenny.

"Why would she worry? You aren't gonna tell her I'm feeding you ice cream before supper, are you?" he asked, and the girls smiled.

"Rhys," Chelsie said, growing serious again, "is Mom going to die?"

I held my breath at the sudden change of subject and saw emotion spill over Rhys before he could catch himself. He pulled his sisters into his arms and whispered into their hair, "I don't think that's happening. Your mom is young and strong. Now, enough of that. Let's call her and cheer her up. Tell her about your new friend and the new coloring books Xander brought."

"What coloring books?" Jenny looked over at the table, jumped up, and ran to where the coloring book and crayons sat. "Cool, it's when Mando took on…." I didn't understand the rest of the statement.

From her description, it was a coloring book with a theme from one of the episodes. Apparently, if I were going to impress the sisters of the man I was crushing on, I needed to watch those shows. Guess I'd be streaming Disney.

Rhys

LUCY WAS in good spirits when the girls called. They sounded excited as they told her about their day, the new school, their new frilly friend, and then about Xander.

"Xander?" Lucy asked, and I knew I would get twenty questions later tonight when I called with my check-in. But she dropped it for now and even teased out that the little boy they'd befriended wasn't indeed female, so much for my being a modern thinker. I'd have to speak with the teacher and see if his—their... well, I'd need to get the pronouns down—parents wanted to come over and visit.

Just as the girls were hanging up, Dad texted and told me Lucy had another week of treatment. He wondered if it'd be okay for them to stay with me before they had to head back down again.

Of course, I texted back. I knew my aunt would approve of all this.

"This is our family's home, our foundation." I'd heard her say it many times, and now it really was. With Dad's money and help, I'd turned it into a habitable place. It made me happy to think of Lucy convalescing here.

By the time Xander's mom arrived, we were all famished, and the girls had talked to Lucy and Dad long enough that they'd missed the opportunity for ice cream. Oh well, we could walk down to Carter's Store later, and they could buy their favorite. It'd be good to get us all out of the house.

The girls seemed to like Xander and his mother from the beginning. Ellen introduced herself and gave each girl a couple stickers, also of Baby Yoda. Both Xander and his mom seemed to have my sister's number when it came to their interests.

"So, Rhys, are you enjoying working at the hardware store?" Xander's mom, Ellen, asked, bringing me out of my internalized planning for the rest of the evening.

I smiled. "I've enjoyed it more than I thought I would," I admitted. "I noticed you moved the canning supplies into one of those back rooms."

I smiled. "Those back rooms have been wasted. I'm glad Stewie let me have my way with it all."

Ellen chucked. "Son, that man has been over the moon since you started. Not that your aunt wasn't a hard worker. She was, but it was all she could do to manage the customers and keep the dust down while Stewie stocked the shelves. I guess things have slowed down a lot over the years," she said. "At one time that place was busy all the time. Now, well, it's like all of Wilcox. Things have all slowed down a lot."

All the talking stopped when we finally sat down to eat. The lasagna? Oh my goodness, that was delicious. Even my picky sisters barely breathed as they inhaled it.

"Ellen, that was amazing," I said when I sat back and wiped the sauce off my lips.

"Aah, thanks, Rhys. I learned it from old man Marco before he died." She looked nostalgic for a moment, then sighed and got up to start clearing dishes.

"Oh no, don't worry about that. The girls and I have cleanup duty."

My sisters both moaned a put-upon sigh but got up and helped me clear the table.

Because Ellen had done all the work before, it was just washing off the plates and putting them into the dishwasher. Chelsie and Jennie wiped the table down and then took their coloring books and crayons to the coffee table in the living room.

I just shook my head and thanked all that was good that I'd bought a glass table that could easily be wiped down to remove errant crayon marks.

Xander

I STARED AT the little house across the street from Rhys. I hadn't even noticed the land it backed up to. Most of it was unusable because the river bent here, causing the bank to be unstable. Over the years, it'd washed the land away and created a gully.

Mom told me the guy who owned it was moving out of town and wanted to sell it and the surrounding land. They wanted too much for it, of course. It was a holiday home, which brought in income, and everyone who owned those properties these days thought they had a five-star hotel.

But the land was interesting. I didn't hesitate. I offered a realistic price, which the owner luckily accepted. Now I had to secure the land and extend my small housing project to this side of the river.

It also solved the land purchase issue around Rhys because I could donate land on this side of the bridge for a park.

As I walked around the neighborhood, I saw several homes backed up to a large undeveloped parcel of land between them and the creek. The houses had been built just after World War II. Small and not very well made, they had been mostly rental property for years. If I could get my hands on them, I'd have a valid project that would make Wilcox much more desirable.

Would Rhys hate it? I had no idea. Maybe. Yet a community of new homes with historical architectural elements in mind meant the value of his house would improve, and it had to be better than having run-down rental homes across the street.

I'd have to discuss it all with him, but I couldn't put energy into that project right now. There was just no way I'd have time. I needed to focus on the project in front of me. I needed to get the land purchased, and since my mom was the main Realtor in town, I figured she'd be able to let me know if that was possible.

I saw Rhys's dad and stepmother climb out of the car as I was surveying the property. I didn't hesitate. I knew she was probably tired, but I wanted to meet them sooner rather than later.

"Hi, are you Rhys's family?" I asked.

The woman smiled. "Yes, are you his new boyfriend? Xander?"

I almost swallowed my tongue and must've blushed because she nearly stumbled when she started laughing.

"Ignore her, she's in good spirits and gets ornery when she feels better."

I chuckled. "I'm Xander, yes, and you must be Lucy."

"I am, and this is Rhys's father, Mark. This is fortuitous. We were just discussing you."

"Um, okay. Let me get the door," I said. Although Rhys's stepmom was giving me the business, she was still very weak. His father took her elbow, helped her up the stairs, and winked at me as they passed through the door.

"Rhys, we're here," Mark said as we entered.

"Daddy!" I could hear the squeals of two young girls from the top floor, and within seconds, they were down the stairs and in their parents' arms. Rhys came down a moment later, shaking his head.

"They were doing their homework," he said as Lucy looked up from hugging her daughters.

"Okay, I love you both so much it's pulling my insides out, but your brother said you were doing homework, so you two skedaddle and get that done. When you're finished, maybe we'll all go for pie," she said, which got another squeal out of the girls.

"They are food motivated," Mark said, laughing.

"Like their daddy," Lucy said. Then she turned toward me. "Okay now, let's get to know you."

I laughed as she led me into the living room, and not unlike the ladies of Wilcox, they began to pepper me with personal questions. Coming from a small town, I didn't mind.

But she tired quickly, and after their luggage was brought in by Rhys and Mark, she excused herself to lie down before she had daughter duty.

"How's she doing?" Rhys asked as soon as the door closed on the first-floor master bedroom.

"Amazing, considering all the chemo and radiation she's been through. The new treatment has taken much better than the last time."

Rhys glanced toward the bedroom and then up the stairs. "The prognosis wasn't good from my online search. Dad, is… do they think the treatment will help?"

Mark shrugged, and his age showed on his face for a moment. Like Rhys, he was small and lean. If I met him on the street, I'd guess he wasn't much older than us, but the pressures of having a sick spouse showed heavily on him.

"They won't commit to anything, saying it's too soon, but yeah, she's already done better than I think they expected. We'll just have to wait and see."

Rhys nodded and glanced over at me. "So you survived my stepmother's questioning. Too bad she's the easy one. Wait until my mother gets hold of you."

Mark moaned and shook his head. "Sorry, son, Rhys is correct. You're in for it there. Best just breathe through the pain when it comes around."

I cocked an eyebrow but didn't have time to respond before the twins rushed down, ready for their dinner.

I'd been here more than a few times since the girls moved in, and pizza, tacos, and a plethora of stuff my mother would frown on seemed the norm. When Rhys pulled out a homemade casserole, I cocked an eyebrow. I opened my mouth to respond, but then I got a look from Rhys that couldn't be mistaken for anything other than a warning to keep my mouth shut.

After supper I followed Rhys to the basement to give Mark and Lucy some alone time with the girls. "They're excited to have them home, huh?" I asked.

"Yeah, this has been so hard on them. They don't talk about it much, but they… well, it's hard on all of us."

I glanced at him. "Hey, want to go with me to my friend's house tomorrow? They're on the verge of starting a barn conversion. It's been in planning for a little over a year, and I think it'll be a cool project. I told them I'd stop by."

Rhys smiled. "I have to work at the store tomorrow morning, but only for a few hours. I'm covering for Melinda, who does the Saturday shifts, but I'm free after that."

I leaned over, kissed him, and pushed him onto the sofa. "Wanna spend the night with me?" I asked, and when I rubbed my crotch into his, he moaned.

"Oh yeah, very much so," he said, and I laughed. Since the girls were here, we'd had to settle for a few quickies during the day before he went to pick them up. I hated the house I was about to tear down, but the bed was comfortable, and it'd be more than nice to have him spend the entire night with me—something I'd been thinking about a lot.

Rhys

I ADORED MY family. I knew how lucky I was to have them, especially my baby sisters. I also didn't mind sharing my home—Aunt Helen's former home—with them. That didn't mean I wasn't missing my privacy. On top of that, having Xander in my bed never happened.

Well, okay, that's not true. We christened my bed the day after I set it up while the girls were at school. But there's a difference between a quickie and a night of passionate lovemaking.

When Xander pushed me back on the sofa and ground into me, I almost creamed myself right then. I missed him so much. Yeah, I was fucking ready to go to his house right then. Unfortunately I knew I couldn't go, just in case Dad and Lucy needed me.

Dad and Lucy would have kid duty all weekend, so I needed to take advantage of the time. If that meant visiting his friends, so be it. Although I'd have preferred just to snuggle and screw around at his place.

I had no idea how well Lucy was or wasn't doing. It wouldn't do to leave them empty-handed.

After Xander left I hung out with them and even got pulled into the visit to the café where Chelsie told Lucy "the best pie in the world was made." By the time we got back, Lucy was fading fast, so she kissed the girls, and then Dad and I hurried them upstairs and got them ready for bed.

When Dad sat down and picked up their favorite book, I disappeared downstairs and was going to turn in myself when Lucy stopped me.

"Hey," she said as I came into the living room.

"Hey yourself. How you feeling?" I asked.

She waved her hand. "I'm doing fine... well, as fine as one can be when they've had poison pumped into their bloodstream. Listen, I wanted to personally thank you for helping with the girls. I—"

She took a couple of breaths to steady herself. I walked over and put my hand on her shoulder. "Lucy, I know, but of course I'd help. You're my family."

She nodded and ignored the tear that slipped down her cheek. "You're a good man, Rhys. Just know how appreciative I am, okay?"

I nodded and was about to turn away when a gentle breeze drifted through the room. No windows were open, and the air wasn't on, so—

"That's your aunt, isn't it?" Lucy whispered.

I laughed. "Probably. She hasn't been around much, but, well, you know how important family was to her. She's probably wanting to keep an eye on you and the girls."

"More likely she wants you to know she's here for you," Dad said as he walked into the room.

Lucy smiled, and another tear slipped down her cheek. "Well, good. We need all the support we can get."

The breeze shifted again, and I noticed then that we'd left the window open in the kitchen. But it didn't matter; we knew in our hearts that Aunt Helen was with us.

"Well, so now that you've got kid duty, I'm going to go sit in my hot tub and then turn in early. Your kids have about worn me out," I said, and both Dad and Lucy laughed.

I hissed happily as I lay back and let the bubbles ease my muscles. I wasn't joking—raising my sisters was a lot of work, and it was stressful. You never knew if you were doing it right. There are so many things happening all at once when six-year-olds are involved.

It made me second-guess ever wanting children—not that I had prospects for being a dad anytime soon. Hell, I hadn't had any relationships last long enough even to discuss the matter. I wondered what Xander thought of kids.

I got out of the hot tub. "Cart before the horse," I said quietly as I dried off. I didn't need to think about domestic life with a man I'd barely begun to see, even if he *had* been a frequent visitor since we'd first hooked up. Even if my sisters adored him and his mother. Even if his mother made me laugh, and I loved having them around when they came over together. That was just my innate need for family, for connection. Something I clearly got from my sweet aunt Helen.

Aunt Helen. I really liked the idea that she was still with us, even if it was only in spirit. Lucy needed her. I don't know why I knew that, but I did. There is something significant about the connections between this world and the next, and it felt important to believe Aunt Helen might be on that side, prompting Lucy's recovery.

That woman needed to survive because, as much as I loved my father, he needed Lucy to help those girls grow up and be the incredible women I could already tell they would be. Just like Aunt Helen had stepped in when I needed her to be a surrogate parent for me.

Mom and Dad were great parents, that's not what I mean, but when they were going through their divorce... well, I needed that—needed her. I knew I was playing the same role for Chelsie and Jenny, but I wasn't Aunt Helen. I was too selfish and lazy.

Hell, since they'd been here, I'd fed them pizza and hamburgers, and only forced them to eat broccoli a few times—and then only because Xander's mom brought it over. No, Lucy needed to survive because I wasn't any better at this than Dad was. Not that I should be. Damn it, I was their brother, not their surrogate parent. Brothers are supposed to feed you crap food, right?

Sure, I thought, but I forced them to do their homework, and their teacher was pleased with how well they'd adjusted in school. So I could pat myself on the back for that much, at least.

Xander

I HAVE NO idea why I was so excited for Rhys to meet my bestie, Brandon. Before Cliff, I'd have been jealous because he and I liked the same type of guys. Not that Cliff, his husband, had given me the time of day. In fact just a little flirting had put him off.

I'd spent a lot of time bridging the gap between us since our first meeting, and luckily, we were buddies now. Not that I got to spend much time with them.

As planned, I drove to the hardware store, picked Rhys up, and then drove us to the farm. "So, tell me about these guys," Rhys asked.

"Well, Brandon has been one of my best friends since elementary school. His mom and dad are the doctors in town. Well, his mom is a nurse practitioner, and his dad's a doctor, but same thing. Cliff is his husband, recently married. Cliff moved here from California when the fires took his home."

"Oh, that's tough," Rhys said.

"Yeah, it was hard on him. Anyway, I used to help out at the dairy across the street. I don't think Levi will be there, since he's a teacher and will probably be grading papers today, and Keya, his wife, is busy working on their new vineyard, but Levi grew up at the dairy. He's another of our friends."

"Cool," Rhys said. "Wait, Levi Owens?" he asked.

I looked over at him. "Yeah, do you know him?"

Rhys laughed. "Very well. We had a couple of classes together. He's older than me. I was only a freshman when you and he were seniors, but Levi was the class clown. He sorta took me under his wing. I was new here and didn't have many friends. Levi helped change that by hanging out with a gangly first-year student."

"That'd be Levi. Good guy deep down. Brandon's the same. He and I played football, so that's probably why you never met him. You know, I remember you from high school, though."

Rhys looked at me. "Oh, I remember you too. I might have had a little crush, but I'll never admit that."

I leaned back and laughed. "I think you just did. Truth is, I thought you were cute back then, but we ran in totally different circles. I also thought the age difference might cause problems."

"I came out when I was really young, like nine or something. My parents were always supportive, but I didn't have a boyfriend until I was in my twenties. Even then, my parents only met him once. It would've been cool to date when I was in high school, and dating a senior football star would've really elevated my popularity status."

I pulled his hand over and kissed it. "You just wanted me as an influencer, then?"

"Oh." He slipped his hand out of mine and slowly slid it down to my crotch. "I'm sure I could've found other uses for you as well."

I swallowed hard and moved his hand away from my cock. We were just about to meet my buddies, and a raging hard-on would not be a good idea.

Rhys just laughed, leaned over, and kissed my cheek. "Just so you know, I'm really looking forward to spending the night with you."

"Yeah, okay, so this will be a short visit," I said in a voice slightly higher than usual.

We pulled up to the construction trailer Brandon and Cliff were still using, and I cringed. I felt bad for them still in that thing, but they'd somehow made it work. I forced myself to think of liver and onions to hopefully make my aching cock calm down.

Brandon came out to greet us, and I was at least soft enough to not embarrass myself too much. "Hey, Brandon, how you doing?" I pulled my friend into a hug.

Cliff came out after him, and I did the same with him. "Brandon, Cliff, this is Rhys. Rhys, Brandon and Cliff."

Rhys smiled and shook their hands. "Oh, I remember you from high school," Brandon said. "You're the cute guy Levi was convinced I needed to marry."

"What?" Rhys and I asked at the same time.

Brandon laughed. "I'd just come out to Levi, and he was convinced Rhys was the only other gay guy in town, so naturally, he wanted to fix us up."

"Wait," Cliff said behind him. "I thought he wanted to fix you up with me."

"Oh, he did. When he found out you were gay, then all his focus shifted to you."

Rhys chuckled. "I sorta remember him playing matchmaker. But not too hard, though. I was pretty shy back then."

"Well, now you're going out with this piece of lead?" Brandon bumped me playfully.

"We're fooling around, at least," Rhys said and winked at me.

"Fooling around." I had to think of liver and onions again to not get hard at the thought of fooling around with him again.

"Hey, why don't you take us to the barn and show us your latest plans?" I said as I all but led the way. The sooner we got this over with, the sooner I could get Rhys back to my place for that fooling around.

We walked through the cleaned-out barn. "When did you clean everything out?" I asked.

"Oh, a few weeks ago. A contractor agreed to take the project on, but then they fell through. We're looking again," Brandon said and winked at me.

"No, don't start. I've already told you that me working for you as a contractor is a bad idea. I prefer to remain friends."

"Ah, come on. It's not like we haven't argued before. And you have all those crews, and your job is over. It's perfect timing."

"No. Now show me the latest plans," I said to force him off the subject. I'd worked on enough projects to know that building your friend's place was the last thing you wanted to do if you wished to remain friends. Contractors dropped hard news on people all the damned time. It would be bad.

Add to that the complexity of a barn conversion. *No, just no.*

I smiled as they opened the detailed blueprints and showed me their final improvements. "Wow, guys, this is going to be amazing. Beyond amazing."

"If we can hire the right contractor. Do you know how many we've talked to that just weren't right?" Cliff asked.

I sighed. "Yeah, it's tough out there these days. I mean, I'm working to do the project in Wilcox, and I'm begging this guy to take on the project management." I said, pointing at Rhys. Then the bell went off in my head.

I didn't say anything, because I didn't want to put Rhys on the spot, but I'd done some research online and seen some of the construction projects that he and his father had done.

"You'll have to get a foundation poured in here," he said.

He studied the plans for several moments before he added, "That's the hardest part, if you want my opinion. We did one of these in Salem, bigger than this one. It was a project for one of the vineyards up there, but I'm telling you now, jacking every support post up and out of the ground so you can pour a concrete base is a lot. Unless you plan to build a basement. That could be even worse."

"You've done a barn conversion?" Cliff asked.

Rhys nodded. "Well, not me. My father did, but I helped him on the project. Truth be known, we did a couple, but I wasn't on the other projects. My dad could probably advise you who would be good to take this on."

"Why not you? Or your dad?" Brandon asked, and Rhys smiled.

"Well, one, because I'm not a project manager, which I've told this one a few hundred times now. My dad would probably love it, but he's pretty tied up right now."

"Well, we'd appreciate any help you can give," Cliff said.

"Do you mind if I borrow your blueprints? I can take them to him and have him look them over. If a contractor in the vicinity can do it, he'd know."

"Man, that would be amazing," Brandon said.

We spent half an hour or so hanging out but turned down their invitation to the Owenses' for dinner. "Well, at least come over this Sunday evening. I'm making a roast, and Sue's agreed to make her famous homemade ice cream. It should be fun."

"You're cooking?" I asked Brandon, who gave me a cockeyed look.

"Dude, I can cook. Just not in here." He pointed at the tiny construction trailer.

"Yeah." I cringed. It would be hard to live in this place all this time. I looked at Rhys, who shrugged. "I'm game if you're sure it's okay," I replied.

"I'll ask, but I think it'll be fine. Rhys?" he asked.

"Sure, if I'm not needed at home," he said as Cliff handed him the blueprints.

"Okay, well, we'll see you then," I replied. Then we climbed into my vehicle and headed down the road.

"Well, what'd you think?" I asked, causing Rhys to smile.

"I think you've got nice friends, and that barn conversion, if they get it off the ground, will be amazing."

"Yeah, do you really think your dad will know someone?" I asked.

"Oh yeah, but between you and me, he won't be able to keep his hands off it. My guess is he's going to want to manage it." He paused and sighed. "Provided he won't be too busy with Lucy."

I reached over, took his hand, and squeezed. "Well, maybe it's time for you to take over that role for him, you know… since you've done these before."

Rhys just shook his head, but he leaned closer to me without responding. He didn't say no, which was a total win for me.

Rhys

DAMN, I WANTED to do it. That barn conversion was going to be freaking awesome. The project in Salem was the only one I'd asked my dad to let me work on. Usually I took projects as they came. At first he refused, saying he needed me in Portland, but I put my foot down, and he didn't fight me. Instead he took the lead himself, and he and I had a great time working side by side. In the end, that's exactly what it needed. That project was one major headache after another, and he didn't make any money on it. Had we not been on the project ourselves, it would've cost him a fortune.

We drove back to Xander's place, and I would've excused myself to go and tell Dad about the project, but before I could leave, Xander pulled his shirt off and pushed me down on his couch. "I'm going to fuck you into tomorrow," he said.

Xander was rough, which was exactly what I needed after all the family stress. We stripped as we walked, and before I had my legs up in the air, Xander's fingers were probing my ass, prepping me. He sucked my cock as his fingers found all my happy spots; then he lubed up and slipped inside.

"Fuck, yes, fuck," I yelled, enjoying the freedom his empty house gave us.

I watched with pure happiness as he took me again and again. I ended up pushing Xander onto his back and climbing onto his big muscular body before he slipped inside me again. When I came, I arched back and brought Xander over the edge with me.

I collapsed onto his chest, content and happy. How could a roll in the hay, or in this case, on Xander's ugly couch, make me so relaxed?

He snored quietly as I lay on his shoulder, and I don't think I'd ever felt so content. He touched all my soft spots when we were like this. He also knew how to quiet my brain.

I rolled over, looked up at the ceiling, and felt the quiet surround me as I fell asleep, completely and utterly at peace.

Xander

"Mom?" Rhys all but yelled. Then he dropped my hand and ran into his mom's embrace as I stood, paralyzed, outside his house.

My mother used to watch reruns of an old show called *Dynasty*. Mom said she and her mother watched it together when she was young. I don't remember much about the show other than Joan Collins's character. Alexis was as intimidating as hell.

Rhys's mother reminded me of Alexis—well put together in a way that demanded respect without lifting a very well-manicured eyebrow.

"Mom, this is Xander, my… well, my friend."

His mom smiled slightly as she looked my way. "Xander, this is my mother, Linda, and her husband, Johney."

"It's a pleasure to meet you, Xander." She studied me momentarily, then smiled brightly, an expression that completely changed her features. I could see Rhys in her face. "Lucy told me you were handsome, but she didn't tell me you were *this* handsome," she said.

Two things shocked me. First, that Lucy, Rhys's stepmother, had told her anything, and second, that she complimented my looks.

"Um, thanks," I stumbled, and she just laughed.

"Okay, well, we just got here. Your father said he thought you had room for us. If not, we can stay in the hotel down the street." She looked at Rhys.

"Oh no, I've got room. But Mom, why didn't you call?"

"I did, honey. You didn't answer, and we wanted to come check on Lucy."

Rhys looked at his phone and sighed. "I must've turned it off. Okay, come on in."

I followed them into the house and smiled as Linda hugged Lucy like a long-lost friend. Then the girls bounced down and called out for Aunt Linda and Uncle Johney. My mind was blown.

"Bring your stuff down to the lower level," Rhys said. "You can stay in my bedroom down there. I'll take the upstairs."

"Or you can stay with me," I quickly said, causing the entire room to look at us.

I blushed under the group's attention, and Rhys snickered. "Sure, that's probably a great idea. Mom, Johney, you can stay in my room downstairs."

After my blustering, I was able to sit back and enjoy the afternoon with Rhy's family. Lucy wasn't feeling great, so she took several naps. The girls bounced between the adults, including me. When I got a call from my mother, I walked into the kitchen to answer.

"Hey," I said.

"Hey yourself. When are you going to come over? I expected you last night. Friday nights are our time."

"Oh, sorry, Mom, Rhys's dad and stepmother came in yesterday, and I got carried away with that."

"Is she doing okay?" Mom asked, concerned.

"I think so. She seems to be doing well."

"Is that your mother?" Lucy asked, startling me and causing me to almost drop the phone.

"Um, yeah."

"Oh, please ask her to come join us for dinner. I want to meet her and thank her for helping with the girls. Besides, Linda brought all the makings for her delicious shrimp Provençal. She always makes too much."

"I most certainly do not. I make just enough, but yes, Xander, son, please invite your mother. I'd love to meet her."

I swallowed hard, knowing instinctively this wouldn't be good for me. "Um, Mom. Rhys's family want you to come over tonight. They're having some kind of shrimp dish."

"Shrimp Provençal, my father was French," Linda said.

"Oh wow," my mother responded. "Yes, I'd like that very much."

I put the phone on speaker and let the women plan when and what Mom should bring. When they hung up, Linda pinned me with a look. "So, Xander…," she began, and I knew the inquisition was upon me. "I hear you worked for a large construction company."

"Yes, ma'am, I did. But I left a few weeks ago. I'm working on my own project now."

"Really? What kind of project?" she asked.

Rhys and his dad walked in behind the women and sat at the large counter in his kitchen as I explained that I'd be tearing down the house I was living in and would begin building houses along that side of the river.

"Really? Are you going to manage it yourself, or will you hire a manager?" Mark asked.

I glanced at Rhys, who immediately rolled his eyes. "Well, honestly, I was hoping to recruit your son."

"And I've already said I'm not a manager."

"But you could be," Mark countered.

"I could be a lot of things, but I'm not. Now, Mom, about that shrimp Prov—"

"Oh no, not quite yet. I still have to get to know this handsome young man you're seeing. Before that, though, I want to know more about this project of his. You know, Xander, we're a family obsessed with all things construction. You already know Rhys and his father are in the business, but Johney here is an architect, and I've managed more than a few projects myself."

I grinned. I didn't know Rhys's mom had been involved, but now that I did, it didn't surprise me. "That's cool. I fell into the business at a young age, but I love it. I hope to expand into the commercial side eventually and help rebuild Wilcox."

I blinked when I realized I'd confessed a dream that I hadn't even shared with my own mother. For some reason, sharing that with this family felt right. With Rhys's family.

"That's ambitious, but if you've done that with your former employer, I suspect you're qualified enough," Mark said, which, for some reason, made me feel prouder of my background than normal.

"Thanks, sir. There's a lot of hurdles to cross. I'm on the county's bad side at the moment. My buddy Levi and I painted a couple of the historic bridges next to his home, and although we used historic colors and my ancestors built the bridges, it made the county mad. In fact, if it weren't for your aunt Helen, well, it could've been worse.

"Really?" Mark asked. "Tell us more."

I smiled at the memory, then described the night Helen Healy put the pompous politician in his place, how she all but told the man to sit down and be quiet, how she commanded the meeting and drew laughs from her family.

"This sounds just like her," Linda said.

"We all adored Aunt Helen," Rhys admitted, and for a moment, I thought about telling them about the journal and what I'd learned about her and my aunt Greta. But it didn't seem right, so I put my arm around Rhys and drew him to me instead.

The family seemed to notice the affection, especially when Rhys leaned into me, and they all quickly dispersed.

"Thanks for telling us about our aunt. Her loss still weighs heavily on us. We were all so close," he whispered.

"I love how your family is so connected," I said. "I'm guessing your aunt Helen had something to do with that?"

Rhys face lifted. "Yeah, when my mom and dad divorced, I came to live here with Aunt Helen, and she forced both my parents to come down for frequent visits. Of course, that just deepened the bond between her and Mom.

"Then, when Dad married Lucy, Aunt Helen sat them both down and told them something. I wasn't there, but whatever it was, it seemed to click for both women. They've been friends ever since."

I hugged him and kissed his temple as he relived the memories of his aunt. "I met her, you know, right before she passed away. I came over for a visit."

I felt a prickle in the air and somehow knew I shouldn't say more. "I… well, I liked your aunt a lot. She was a great woman."

"She was, and as you can see, she had a major impact on each of us."

Rhys and I walked into the living room, where everyone was gathered. Thankfully, the questions from Rhys's mom seemed to have subsided for now.

"Hey, Dad, would you have time to see a project Xander's friends are about to start? I told them I'd ask if you knew a team of contractors who could do the job for them," Rhys asked, surprising me.

"Sure. Honey, are you feeling okay enough for me to go with Rhys and Xander?"

"Yes, please, Rhys, get this man out from under my feet," Lucy said.

"Xander, do you think Brandon and Cliff would mind if we drove by?"

"Wow," I said. "Better than that—I think they'll give you the tour. Let me call."

I quickly rang Brandon, and I could tell he was excited. "Sure, we'll meet you at the house in, like, thirty minutes. Is that long enough for you to get here?"

"Sure," I said, knowing the drive only took half that time.

I told them what Brandon had said and nudged Rhys as thanks for the opportunity. If anyone could come up with a qualified crew, I had to assume it was Rhys's father, Mark.

Rhys

I KNEW I was playing a hand when I asked Dad to come to see the barn conversion, but I hadn't thought of much else since I'd seen it. Well, at least when Xander wasn't loving on me. The man had a way of forcing all thoughts out of my head when he was working me over.

I wanted that project, and even though I knew Lucy was sick and Dad shouldn't be doing a project, I felt pretty confident I could pull it off if I had his help. But I didn't want to say that or even allude to it until I knew Dad could at least help me out.

We drove over in Xander's truck, and the first thing we saw when we pulled in was the construction trailer. Neither of us were strangers to those, but for real, it wasn't a good first impression.

Brandon and Cliff met us as we pulled in, and although my father was an expert at schooling his expression, I could feel the excitement coming from him when he spotted the barn.

I'd forgotten I'd brought the blueprints with me until Xander pulled them out from the back seat of his truck. Brandon and Cliff explained what they wanted to do with the barn as we walked through. Then Xander handed Dad the blueprints, and he rolled them out in the same place I'd seen them the day before.

Dad didn't say anything, just looked over the plans. All of us stood around him as he considered them.

Finally he sighed. "Rhys and I have done one of these together. I assume he told you of the nightmares associated with a build like this."

I shook my head. "No, I wanted someone with more experience than me to explain all the pitfalls," I replied, and Dad nodded.

"Well, barn conversions have three distinct phases. The first and most important could end the entire project before it starts, and that's the foundation."

I couldn't help but smile as Dad explained each step meticulously. Finally he sighed. "If you want my honest opinion, after looking over your barn, I see issues—issues that will cost you more than the building is worth. I wouldn't recommend a traditional build on this structure. Here, let me show you," Dad said. I had to resist looking at the faces of the men, as I could only guess how disappointed they must be feeling with Dad's likely accurate observations.

"You'll see there's significant termite damage here, on this major support post. I also noticed significant wood rot as well. Some wet rot, some dry. Regardless, all those beams have to be replaced, and since they were likely built using virgin timbers, you won't be able to replace them, at least not as they are."

"So the project is doomed?" Cliff asked, and despair encircled him.

"No, in fact, I don't think it's doomed at all, but if I were your contractor, I'd tell you that you *can* do this responsibly and affordably. You just have to think outside the box."

I knew where Dad was going. We'd done a teardown of an ancient general store in a tiny town not far from here. The place had been about to fall in. We took the old building apart, saved all the good materials, and rebuilt what looked almost exactly like the old building, but with new materials accented by the old.

As Dad explained that process to the guys, I watched their despair turn to excitement. "So it's basically a new building, but it looks exactly like the old barn?"

"Yes, and you've got some issues right here in your loft. See, these rooms aren't big enough for code. If you expand the building two feet on either side as well as the back, well, you'll end up at code, and no one will be the wiser."

"Oh man, that's so cool," Brandon said, and for a moment, I thought he might hug my dad. Instead, he turned and hugged Cliff.

"You're hired," Brandon said, causing Dad to chuckle.

"Oh, boys, I'd love to, but my life doesn't allow that. But I'm guessing my son might be willing to take this on. Otherwise, I doubt he'd have dragged me out here."

"Dad," I said, frustrated he'd given me away. I shrugged. "Yeah, I'd like to do it. It's so cool to do a barn conversion. I would've loved to have done that for you, but Dad's right, the integrity of the building is jeopardized by rot and termite damage. We can get that treated, though. Then we'll pull the building down, preserve the good timbers, and make something truly amazing when we're done."

Cliff hugged me. "I can't believe it. We've finally found a contractor we want." Then he turned and kissed Brandon.

"Okay. I'll have my guys send you the contracts. Rhys, we can discuss which crews you can pull down here to help. I've got a few guys who live not too far from here and travel up to Portland to work. I'm sure they'd like to have work closer to home."

"Perfect, Dad, thanks," I said.

We spent another hour or so reviewing the blueprints and discussing how they'd have to change. "How attached are you to your architect?" Dad asked.

"Um, we hardly know them. It was a company out of Eugene. They were okay, though, I guess."

"I usually recommend my guy. He's part of my family, sort of. I could drop these off with him. Coincidentally, he's here in Wilcox for the next few days. I'm sure he could rework what you've got to reflect the changes we need to make."

Brandon and Cliff exchanged glances and then nodded. "Can we meet him?" Cliff asked.

Dad smiled. "Of course. I'll talk to him tonight, and Rhys, can you tell them what he says tomorrow?"

I nodded. Though I might be on lead, this was every bit my father's project—exactly as I'd hoped it would be. Dad didn't have much time with Lucy sick, but he could use a distraction, and I was sure I could pull off most of the work. I just needed to know I had him in my corner if I needed him.

I glanced over at Xander and was immediately struck by the fact that I had him as well. From my surreptitious research of Xander, he was also an expert in our field. He'd been on more than one magazine cover when he led projects. Between Dad and Xander, I was confident we could pull this conversion—well, new build—off.

That excited me.

Xander

MARK AND Lucy left the following Monday to return to the cancer treatment center in California. Johney and Rhys's mom, Linda, stuck around, mostly because Johney took to the barn project like a duck to water.

I loved watching him work with the guys, and he was great with customers. I knew my architect, a ninety-year-old man who still operated out of an old downtown building, would have to retire soon. He was still spry, but even he eventually had to surrender to the ravages of time.

I'd initially gone with him because I liked him. He was smart, funny, good at what he did, and the town respected him. If he got behind a plan, the city tended to as well.

But now that Johney was an option, I'd be using him to help with my plans, so I called my guy and asked if Johney could stop by and look at what we were doing.

The moment they saw each other, they laughed, clapped their hands, and bro hugged. It was a bit odd to see a man as old as Joe, my architect, do a bro hug. "You're still practicing, Joe? I figured you and Mary would be down in Florida fishing off some pier."

"Oh no, son, my roots go too deep in Wilcox to leave. You still married to that pretty Linda?"

"Oh yeah, going on ten years now."

I listened as the two reminisced. Then Joe turned his attention to the site plan, and I tried not to smile so hard it hurt.

"Oh, you've outdone yourself." Johney said, "This will be beautiful. I want to get over there and see the land now."

When Johney suggested a couple of changes, I almost thought Joe would go after him. Instead, he studied the suggestions, agreed with him on one or two things, and marked the paper.

"Now, Johney, you're not a young buck. You know that will…." Then he went off on a tangent about all the potential problems.

Joe and Johney left to get a beer, basically dismissing me, which I was one hundred percent okay with. I knew how to read architectural plans, but my head was swimming with all the acronyms the two men kept throwing at one another. I was happy to take my leave and let them work out any details.

I suspected I could easily pull Johney onto my team. With the two of them on my side, maybe they could rescue me if any concerns were raised at next week's council meeting.

Concerns. The council had returned my proposal faster than I hoped. They were negative in their first review, and there were a lot of questions that Joe said were, "Bullshit. They don't have a clue what they're talking about."

I chuckled. "No, they're still upset about Levi and me painting those bridges."

"More likely they're upset 'cause Helen put them in their place. Too bad she's not still here to whip them into shape again," he said.

"Too true," I lamented, but I wasn't ready to give up. I'd answered all their concerns and would respond to them at the council meeting. If I could just tie Rhys down as my project manager, that would go a long way to help me secure my application as well.

Not that I thought I wouldn't get approval. I would. They didn't have a good reason to turn me down, but that didn't mean they couldn't make my life a living hell with inspections that nitpicked everything we did.

I could pull some strings. Mom, for example, could be influential. I was sure Stewie and Joe could help too. But I preferred to wow the council, get them fully behind me, and then maybe, just maybe, I could get the project done.

Rhys returned to his place and stayed in the upstairs bedroom next to the girls while his mom and Johney stayed on the lower level, which I could attest they loved. Of course, what wasn't to love? The basement was amazing. It was rugged, definitely not as formal as the upper floor, but it screamed Rhys.

I almost thought Linda would prefer formal, but on more than one occasion, she and Johney had taken to the hot tub, and we had to share it with them in the evenings when I came over.

It wasn't romantic, of course, but it was still nice. Mom even joined us once after we'd had a huge meal together and gotten the girls off to sleep. How could it be so right in such a short time?

Our families meshed like they'd always been together. The fact that I was beginning to get serious about Rhys certainly made that feel even more significant.

One night, right before I headed back to my place, we were all seated around the dining room table. The girls had finished their meal and were kneeling around the coffee table in the living room, coloring.

Rhys and I held hands as Mom and Linda talked about a social program here in Wilcox. Rhys's mom had agreed to help with it, since she and Johney were going to spend another week here to help with the girls.

I glanced over at Rhys, and my heart skipped a beat. He was smiling at something Johney had just said, and at that moment, it was like a light turned on. I was falling in love with Rhys, and I hadn't seen it coming. I mean, yeah, I liked him. I liked him a lot.

Even if we weren't lovers, we'd have easily been friends. But there was so much more to it than that. I wanted Rhys in my life. I shook my head, knowing it was too early to think that way. We were just learning to be lovers and hadn't even announced ourselves as boyfriends.

But I didn't want anyone but him. Rhys had filled my entire life, and I liked that a lot. When he glanced at me, his smile wavered, probably because of my expression. So I smiled, leaned over, and kissed him.

"Want me to take sister duty?" I asked. It was time for the girls to get ready for bed.

"Sure. Girls, head up and get ready. Xander said he'll read to you tonight."

"Really? Will you read *Mandalorian*?" Chelsie asked.

"It's a comic book. Mom bought them," Rhys explained.

"Sure, but only if you're in bed in five minutes. Starting… now!" I said, mimicking how Rhys did it to motivate them.

The girls scurried off while I cleaned up the crayons and put them and the books in the little box Rhys kept under the coffee table. I knew he usually wanted them to clean up after themselves, but it seemed easier to have them go to bed without their usual griping than to have them do a chore I could do in seconds.

Rhys winked at me as I headed up to read *Mandalorian* to the girls. They were both tucked in bed when I got there, and I laughed when Jenny handed me the comic book.

I sat down, opened the first page, and began to read, showing them the pictures like Rhys did when he read to them. It only took a moment before the girls started to doze off, so I marked the page with their unicorn bookmark and was about to leave when Chelsie asked, "Are you going to marry Rhys?"

I chuckled. "Why? Did he say he wanted to marry me?"

They both shook their heads. "No, but he likes you. I think you should marry him and let us be the maids of honor."

"Both of you?" I asked, and they nodded. "Well, that sounds like something to discuss with your brother. Now go to sleep or I'm going to tell him you want liver for supper tomorrow night."

"Blah," the girls said in unison, and I laughed as I left them to fall asleep.

I was always surprised by how quick those two girls were. They seemed to notice what most of us missed. They'd somehow figured out I had feelings for their brother even before I fully acknowledged it.

When I came down the stairs, Rhys and Johney were in a major discussion about metal roofs versus shingles and how each functioned in the Pacific Northwest.

I leaned over, kissed the top of his head, and told him I'd see him tomorrow.

He got up, saying, "The metal roofs have a much longer life span than the shingles, and I still think they're less likely to get algae."

Johney laughed as Rhys turned to me and kissed me good night. "Night, handsome," he said.

"Night," I replied, resisting the urge to tell him I loved him. So weird. What had gotten into me?

I dashed across the bridge and crawled into bed before I said something stupid. I thought about when and where I'd finally make my confession. I hoped he didn't freak out when I did.

Rhys

"SORRY, DAD, no time," I said when he came in asking for me. Stewie had sent him to the loading dock, where I was trying to manage a shipment of lumber. At least a third of the stock was broken, and I had to tag it and send it back before the truck left.

"Hey, no problem. I have good news, though. I'll wait inside with Stewie ."

"Yeah, great," I responded, distracted as the delivery guy threatened to leave.

"Dude, if you drive off, I swear to all that's good, I'll never order from your company again."

Luckily that shut him down, and he slumped against his truck door, pouting. I didn't mind him pouting, but I would mind being stuck with this bullshit shipment.

It took me another half hour before I had all the damaged stuff tagged for the dude to reload. It took an extra half hour to take stock of what we kept. I snapped pictures of the merchandise and sent them to the store email. Aunt Helen had set it up before I got here, since most of our orders had to be done electronically.

I would have to come back later and bring the stuff in. I had already called my helpers, Louis and Jeffrey, to ask them to stock everything this afternoon before the rains set in, and they both said they were free. I needed to talk to Stewie about hiring them at least part-time, since we were increasing our inventory. I didn't have the time or interest to work full-time, and besides, I didn't want to haul crap in and out all day.

Since I started working here, the profit margins had increased over a hundred percent, which made me feel better about asking. It took a bite of his profits, but if I had my way, we'd be increasing that bottom line even more, so we needed to bring them in.

When I walked to the front desk to tell Stewie I'd be in the office, I saw my dad. "Hey, Dad, you're still here?"

"Oh hey, son, yeah, Stewie and I have been talking business. Do you have a moment? I want to take you for a beer. I've got good news."

"Um, no, not really. I have to deal with this crap shipment and—"

"Oh son, go on. You were supposed to be off an hour ago, and I saw Jeffrey drive in. He and that kid will have things put away in no time."

I sighed. Since Lucy and Dad were back, I figured I'd have time to deal with the email later at home. "Okay, well, I guess. I told Jeffrey to store any extra lumber in the plant area. Is that okay?"

"Yeah, son, that's perfect. Now go on, spend some time with your dad."

I laughed. "Yes, sir," I said and saluted him.

Since the hardware store was only a few blocks from our favorite little bar, we decided to walk. "Well, so what's the good news?"

Dad looked over and smiled. "I'd rather wait until we're seated to tell you."

"Oh… okay," I said, not sure how I felt about that.

When the old woman at the bar saw us, she waved, got Dad's typical Bud on tap and my Bud Light in the bottle, and handed them to us. "Thanks." Dad winked at her, and we went to our typical spot.

"Okay, spill. What's the good news?"

Dad laughed and took a sip of his beer. "The treatment they're doing with Lucy has been working. Like, much better than they hoped. She's got a long way to go, but they said her treatments can be given here at the Wilcox clinic. I guess your friend Brandon's mother, the nurse practitioner here, has oncology training and can administer the drugs."

"Awesome, Dad. Damn, that's a relief."

"Yeah, it is, and, well, I know you don't want us underfoot, but I wonder if you mind if we stuck around. I don't want to drag the girls out of school, and I'd prefer we were closer to Lucy's center in case—"

"Dad, no worries. I like having you all here. It's been fun to spend time with the girls again."

Dad smiled. "Okay, well then, with that settled, the next part. Well, I hope you're not upset."

I cocked my eyebrow. "Dad?"

He sighed. "Okay, well, here goes. I sold the company."

My mouth fell open. My father was so invested in his company it was beyond belief that he'd ever part with it. He'd trade me or the girls before he traded Healy Construction.

"Well, say something," Dad insisted.

"Not sure what to say. Um, what... why?"

Dad leaned back, took a deep breath, and let it out slowly. "Son, I was offered a huge sum for the business five years ago. I didn't take it, but I considered it even then. I'm getting older, and I have two daughters, and a wife who has cancer. I regret not raising you. I know you had Aunt Helen, and that was the right choice for you at the time, but even then, I knew my work was interfering with my duties as a father and husband. Well, luckily I've learned from the past. I don't want to repeat the same mistakes." I continued to stare in stunned silence. Finally, he shrugged. "You're upset, aren't you?"

"No, why would I be upset? I'm shocked and bewildered, but no. Not upset."

"Well, it... you've put a lot into that company too. I figured you expected to inherit it one day."

I couldn't help the snort that snuck out. "Dad, that was your dream, not mine. I didn't want to run a huge construction company. I kept telling you that. I like a simpler life, like I have here. In fact, I'm thinking about buying Stewie out."

I stopped short, not intending to say that out loud, and the way my father looked told me I'd probably spoken out of turn.

"Um, well," Dad said. "Okay, don't get mad."

I looked at him askance. "Why would I get mad?"

"Well, because I can't just hold on to the money I got, I'll need to reinvest."

"You offered to buy the hardware store from Stewie, didn't you?"

Dad smiled a fake smile and shrugged. "Yeah, but I didn't know you wanted it."

I leaned back in my chair and laughed loud enough that people turned to see what was up.

"Well, great minds and all that. Or is it that the apple doesn't fall far from the tree? Okay, well, cool. That's good."

"You aren't mad?" Dad asked.

"No, not at all. I just want to see the place keep going, and I knew Stewie wouldn't be able to do it much longer. When we get home,

I'll show you my ideas. I think with just a few minor changes we can increase the bottom line by at least fifty percent, maybe even higher."

"And that's my son!" Dad clapped me on the back.

"Anything else?" I asked, and Dad shook his head.

"Well, okay, maybe."

I cocked an eyebrow at him again. "What?"

"You should take the job with Xander, and before you disagree, let me explain my thinking."

I just stared at him until he stopped chewing his lip and launched into what sounded like a prepared speech. "So, you like Xander, and he likes you. It even looks like it could get serious. I'm going to tell you, after being married to two amazing women, I've learned that when you work as a team and you have a joint venture to keep you focused, it helps. When your mother stopped working for the company, it created resentment. She admitted the same thing. When we were working as a team, we were doing okay. When we stopped, so did the relationship."

"Dad, you and Mom never got along well."

He laughed. "No, that's true enough, but we were a team, and that's the point. Even now, with Johney and me working together as much as we do and her being his manager, it works. Better than when we were married. Lucy is a part of the company. Not always directly, but even now, she knows the ins and outs and even suggested I talk to Stewie about the hardware store. You and I are so much alike, Rhys. You might not want to admit that, but… we work well with a partner."

I took a drink of my beer before I replied, "I know we're alike, Dad, and I'm not ashamed. Why would I be? You're successful and have always done your best by me. I don't know how close Xander and I are. We're new. But I don't know if I want to work for him, not when we're starting to date."

"If it doesn't work out, you can quit," Dad quickly added, "but think about it this way—if you manage his building projects, you can ensure the work across from you is done correctly. No cutting corners that will eventually hurt your property value."

I'd already thought of that, but I wasn't convinced. "I don't know, Dad. It's a lot."

"Yeah." He patted my hand. "But you should seriously consider it. Of course, I'll need you to stay on at the hardware store and help Lucy and me get things set up. Stewie wants to stay on too, but from what I'm guessing, that's more him having a hard time letting go. Regardless, you know what's going on now. If we're going to make it work, I'll need your help."

"Yeah, of course." I stared at my beer. "Dad?" I asked.

"Yeah?"

"What if I'm falling in love with Xander?" I asked. "I mean, I know it's fast, but I've been thinking about him a lot—like, all the time. I've never been in love before. I don't even know if what I'm feeling isn't just lust, you know?"

Dad just laughed. "Oh, son, we can all see you're feeling deeply about that boy, and rightfully so. He seems like a good man. Just take your time. If it's right, you'll know."

I pondered what he said, then decided to launch into what I was most interested in knowing. "Like you and Mom, or like you and Lucy?"

Dad sighed. "I loved your mom, but we were like oil and water. Still are in some ways, but I've always respected the hell out of her. She's smart, witty, and can make even the worst business successful. Lucy? Well, she felt like your favorite clothes. I miss Lucy when I'm gone. I don't know what kind of feelings you have for Xander. Only you can answer that, but let me ask you this—do you argue often?" he asked.

I laughed. "I'm not sure we've had an argument yet."

"See, your mother and I had a blowout argument on our first date." He laughed. "We argued from the time we started dating until we split up."

"And Lucy?"

"Oh, well, we argue, and things were tough a few months back, but no, when I'm not being a stubborn ass, we work through it. And no, to answer your question, we don't argue often. We fit together, Rhys."

Did Xander and I fit together? My mind drifted back to the night I'd spent in his arms. Yeah, we fit together physically, for sure. Mentally? Maybe. I mean, we got along really well, and I enjoyed spending time with him probably more than anyone outside my family.

Okay, I preferred spending time with him more than my family, although it was close.

"Well, shit, Dad. You've given me a lot to think about."

Dad clapped me on the back. "Good. Now tell me those plans. I know Lucy will want to hear, and I'd prefer to do all this before we pick the girls up."

Once my sisters got home, there would only be energy and space to deal with them. Two almost seven-year-old girls were a lot, and my sisters demanded all the attention when they got home.

We walked back to the store, and since I'd walked to work that morning, Dad drove us back to the house. Lucy was in good spirits, having just gotten up from her nap. She had enough energy for me to go over the pro forma I'd written to show Stewie.

I'd been concerned about overwhelming my boss, but now that Dad was looking at it, I wished I'd made it more detailed and included merchandise that I thought we should carry. A considerable part of the store needed to be renovated. I figured I could do most of the work with Jeffrey and Louis. Now Dad was in the picture, it could be done even faster.

"A lot of people come into the store looking for household goods. We could sell a range of things, including soft goods, like towels, soaps, pictures, and cute seasonal things. I've looked up the wholesale costs, and the markup can be as much as three times the original cost. That would bring in an entirely different clientele."

"So you're basically proposing an old-time general store?" Lucy asked.

"I hadn't thought of it that way, but yeah, that's exactly what I'm thinking. Why not expand and take advantage of the space and provide even more of what the community needs?"

Lucy clapped. "Oh, this is perfect, Rhys. I was thinking about similar things, but you've done all the research. Mark, how long would it take you to rebuild the old part of the building?" she asked.

Dad shrugged. "I'll have to go look," he said.

"Not long," I said, smiling. I'd already researched that too. "The roof has to be replaced, and there's rot in one corner. I'm guessing, maybe a month, three weeks if we do it ourselves."

Dad laughed. "I should've known you'd have scoped it out. It seems we have a plan. Shall we bump it off?" He put his fist out, and Lucy and I bumped his. "Okay, we have a plan," Dad said.

"Rhys, can you send me a copy of your proposal? I'd like to write it up in a formal business plan," Lucy asked, and I winked at her.

"Sure thing, oh, and Lucy?" I said. "Congratulations on the treatment. I know you're still fighting it, but well, damn, I'm so happy it's working out."

Lucy got emotional for a moment, and it took her a bit to respond. Finally she leaned over and pulled me into a hug. "Thanks, Rhys, I'm lucky."

"Yeah," I whispered. "We all are."

Xander

"Do you really think I need an attorney at the council meeting?" I asked Jason, the young lawyer who'd helped get Levi and me off the hook for painting the bridges.

Jason shrugged. "I talked to Tim, the other town attorney, about it, and he agrees. The town council will probably try to appease the county, since much of the town's budget comes from them. If you go in there without a strong presence, they'll probably turn you down."

I sighed. "Damn Levi," I said, referring to my friend. "I swear I never thought they'd be so upset over painting a couple of dilapidated old bridges."

"Oh, son, they don't give a damn about those bridges. You, or more accurately, Ms. Healy pissed them off when she put them in their place," Tim said as he came into the conference room.

"Too bad she's not around to push them some more." I seriously missed the older woman.

"No, don't you worry about that. Your family has been in these parts as long as the Healys. That means something to the folks around here. Don't you forget that. However, you might need an advocate to speak on your behalf. That's where Jason or I come in."

I looked at the two men and let out the breath I'd been holding. "Well, shit. Okay. I hoped to do this with honey, not vinegar," I said, repeating something my aunt Greta used to say about catching flies.

"Well, not sure I like being compared with vinegar, but you'll have plenty of time to be sweet. We'll use old Theodore Roosevelt's line and say, when it comes to Wilcox, it's best to speak softly and carry a big stick. We'll be your stick if you need it."

"Got it. Okay."

I showed them what I wanted to do and got appreciative whistles from both men as they saw the blueprints. Like Joe, the architect, they laughed at the ridiculous questions the council had asked me.

By the time we were done, I felt more confident about next Tuesday, the night my proposal was being discussed. Tim said that was also bullshit. "They don't need a public hearing for a residential approval." That confirmed to him they wanted to set it up for me to be turned down. Shit and damn.

Not long ago I had a clear shot at the council's approval. They'd approved of the homes I'd renovated before, but one faux pas and I was chopped liver. It was easy to fall from glory, especially in a small town.

I went directly to Mom's and collapsed in her chair. "What's got you looking so down?" she asked.

"I just left the town attorney's office. He thinks the council is going to give me shit about the development project."

She took a deep breath and shook her head. "Oh, honey, I... well, I've heard they want to turn it down. I'm glad you met with Tim."

"You heard? From whom?" I asked.

"Well, you know Wilcox. They can't keep a secret to save their lives. It's off the record, but old Commissioner Jones still wants to punish you for putting him on the spot."

"Ugh, I wish someone would run for his position and get rid of that pig," I blurted out. Then I glanced at Mom in time to see her blushing.

"Mom?" I asked, and she shrugged.

"Well, that's why I haven't gotten involved. I've already submitted the application to run. Don't tell anyone, though, and for God's sake, don't mention it at the meeting. If they think I'm using my influence as a candidate, they'll chew you up and me with you."

"Oh wow, so should I withdraw my application? I don't want to hurt your chances."

Mom laughed. "No, son. If anything, you should stand up to them. That will make us look strong. Just, you know, don't paint any more public bridges without approval from the county."

I laughed. "Got it. Follow the letter of the law."

She came over and kissed my head. "Okay, come on. I've got burritos in the oven. Why didn't you bring Rhys with you?" she asked.

"Oh, well, that's because he's the busiest person on the planet at the moment."

"And you're missing him?" She hit the mark like always.

"Yeah, Mom. I shouldn't feel like this so fast. I mean, I've only been seeing him for a few months, but already I'm, well, I'm getting attached."

She chuckled. "When you know, you know. I fell so hard for your father. I'd have married him after the first date."

"Ugh, Mom, you and Dad fought like dogs."

"We did because we were both strong-minded, and your father was a little too old-fashioned, and I was a little too liberated to live like a traditional wife. You and Rhys don't seem to have the same issues we did."

I shrugged. "It's too soon to tell, right? I mean, we seem to like the same things—almost too similar, really."

Mom scuffed up my hair. "You're looking for flaws that don't exist. Stop trying to see the wrong and accept the right. If there's issues, they'll show up in time."

I knew she was right. I tended to overthink things, especially with guys I liked.

Since Rhys had agreed to take on Brandon and Cliff's project, he'd been working daily with them. Mark and Lucy were almost ready to close on the hardware store, and they'd already begun planning a significant improvement on that building.

Of course, both projects had already been approved by the county and city planning boards. Mine, not so much. I'd really pissed them off with those bridges. It made me wonder if I'd be better off skipping my plans to redevelop the commercial properties in town.

If the council was against me, I'd never get anything done. I figured time would tell.

It's not like I couldn't do the same thing in various other towns in Oregon, but those towns weren't my home. Nor did they have Rhys, Mom, or my friends Levi and Brandon. I'd just have to see what happened.

Meanwhile, I needed to figure out how to let Rhys know how I felt. If I were lucky, he'd feel the same way.

Rhys

"WE HAVE grave concerns, Mr. Petterson," one of the council members said to Xander. Of course, all I could do was cringe in support.

"Mr. Jones, as Mr. Petterson's attorney, may I ask what your concerns are, specifically?" Tim Bradford chimed in.

The council member regarded Tim for several moments and then looked to his side and eyed the mayor. I could tell they weren't anticipating that Xander would have an attorney present.

"To be honest," Mayor Cliffton said, "you were in trouble with the county just a short time ago for defacing public property."

Tim interjected. "The case was dropped, and the bridges are in much better shape now than they were before. I'm sure you remember. As I recall, you were present, were you not, Mayor Cliffton?"

"Mayor, if this is retribution for something worked out by the county commission and the public who were in attendance that night, I might remind the council that it violates Mr. Petterson's rights. I'm sure that's not the case, though, correct?"

Tim looked at the council over his glasses and pinned the mayor with his glare.

"Tim Bradford, this council is a professional organization, and I expect you to keep your allegations to yourself."

Tim chuckled. "As you wish. Now I repeat, what exactly is the holdup on Mr. Petterson's approval? The house he lives in is a pigsty, which this community has hated for over thirty years. The land next to the covered bridge needs to be upgraded. Mr. Petterson has the financial wherewithal to do the work, and his family is as settled in this town as Ms. Healy, who spoke in front of the county meeting. Why would you not approve this project?"

"Because he has no builder," Kristin Batey chimed in. I didn't know the characters on the council, but I remember Kristin hated my aunt. She was one of the only people who dared stand up to her.

I stood up then and said, "With all due respect, Madam Councilwoman, he does, in fact, have a contractor. We're just finalizing the details."

I don't know what got into me. Maybe it was the council treating Xander so poorly or the fact that Dad's talk had seeped into my head. I made my decision to help at that moment.

"We will need to see your credentials," Kristin said.

"Of course, I'll see that the council has those by morning."

"Did you not just get approval to work on another project here in town, son?" Tim asked.

I felt sick that we were pulling poor Brandon and Cliff into this mess. "Yes, I'm working on a building project already."

"Then your credentials are already on file. Mayor and council members, there is no reason why you can't approve this project tonight, here at the public meeting you've required my client to attend."

I could tell they weren't happy. Unfortunately, that would not help Xander. They scooted away from the mics and spoke for several moments. Finally the mayor came back up to the mic. "We aren't prepared to give that approval tonight, Mr. Healy," he said, calling me by name. "You should submit your paperwork as required for any project. We will consider it and get back to you, Mr. Petterson."

They dismissed the meeting then and disappeared out the back door, clearly not wanting to get into it with any of us.

"Damn," Xander said next to me. "They're digging in their heels."

Tim clapped him on the back. "They're stalling, but unless they can come up with something big, which would be difficult, they don't have any real reason to turn you down. Meanwhile, your mother should alert the community through her network of gossips. I'm sure if people know what is happening, they'll blow a gasket or two."

Tim wasn't wrong, but Xander looked dejected. I put my arm around him and tugged him close, hoping to provide some comfort.

As we drove back to his place, he sighed beside me. "Rhys, they aren't going to approve this. I can feel it in my bones. I've lost all the goodwill I ever had with them. Now… well, I don't know what's next. I need the council behind me to do everything I hoped in Wilcox."

I reached over and took his hand. "I know, but don't give up yet. I heard how Aunt Helen handed the county jerks their asses.

I'm sure someone, probably your mom, will do the same. People in power often have to be reminded that they work for us, right?"

He smiled and squeezed my hand, and I talked him into coming over and sitting in the hot tub with me. Mom and Johney had returned to Portland after Dad and Lucy came home, so we had the hot tub to ourselves. At least I hoped so. Lucy didn't like sitting in it because her skin was tender from all the chemotherapy.

As I suspected, we had the tub to ourselves. I put my foot on his knees as he sat across from me. "So, you're really willing to be my contractor?" he asked, and I laughed.

"Yeah, I think I'd already decided to take it on, but with them being assholes, I didn't want to let them bully you. Besides, Dad says I should."

"Really? Your dad?"

"Yeah, long story, but if you still want me, I'll send my paperwork over to them. Since they already approved it on Brandon and Cliff's build, I can't imagine they'll be able to find fault with my credentials. Besides, if they try, Dad has a lot of Aunt Helen's qualities and will be the first to put them in their place. Hell, he even sounds like Aunt Helen when he starts preaching about family roots and such."

Xander laughed and moved to my side of the tub. "Thank you, Rhys. It means a lot to me. Even if they don't approve me, I appreciate your willingness to help."

I kissed his sexy lips and smiled. "Oh, I have ulterior motives," I said as my hand slid down his muscular torso and wrapped around his clothed cock.

His eyebrow rose, and a sly smile formed on his lips. "Oh, I'm sure we have similar motives in that department."

Xander

RHYS LAY in my arms, all aflush after having sex.

"Rhys?" I asked and waited for him to stir.

"Yeah," he whispered, half asleep.

"I love you," I said and then held my breath.

He turned and looked up at me. Then a smile broke out across his face. "Yeah? I love you too."

"It's too soon, though, right?"

Rhys laughed. "I don't know, but it is what it is." He leaned up and kissed me and then straddled me on the bed. He ran his hand up and down my chest and then leaned over and kissed me deeply. He slowly nuzzled and bit my neck and then did the same to my earlobe.

My cock was beginning to come back to life as he nipped and bit his way down to my groin.

Something had changed with my confession. Our lovemaking was more tender, sweeter, like both of us wanted the other to know how much we cared. I loved having my way with Rhy's body, but making sweet love was almost as rewarding.

The following day, despite the meeting the night before, I was on cloud nine, as Mom always said. No idea what cloud nine was, but I was happier than I'd been in a while.

I'd spent the night in Rhys's bed and really enjoyed it. I loved Rhys Healy, and now he knew. How can you fall in love with someone so much, so quickly? Damn, I had it bad.

Even if the approval came through this week, it would take some time for me to start. I had plenty of savings, but it would be stupid to spend it before my project started. So I needed to find a side job.

I'd just started looking when my phone rang. I hated talking on the phone, and Rhys and Mom only ever texted. If I was getting a phone call, it was either someone trying to get me to buy something or a former client from my previous job, so I ignored it.

I found a few interesting job leads, marked them for later, and was about to go over to Mom's and tell her about last night's hiccup when I remembered the call and opened my voicemail.

Xander, hey, it's Oren. I'm calling on behalf of James Hendrix. He would like to meet with you about how things ended. Can you give me a call?

"Well, I'll be damned," I said out loud. It'd been months since I quit that job. I'd gotten my severance pay and hadn't heard another damned thing. Now all of a sudden....

I groaned as I wondered if this might have something to do with last night's fiasco. I'd better figure it out before whatever was going on bit me in the butt.

"Hey, Oren, It's Xander," I said into the phone.

"Dude, I thought you'd fallen off the side of the earth."

"Um, phones work both ways, dude."

My former assistant chuckled. "True, but I thought you might still be mad, so I didn't want to, you know, upset you more or anything."

"Nah, never mad at you, buddy. What's going on?"

"Well, Mr. Hendrix fired Leon. You probably saw that coming, but he wants to talk to you about coming back."

I threw back my head and laughed.

"No freaking way. I'm in the middle of a new project in my hometown."

"Yeah, I figured someone with your skills wouldn't last long, but I think he'd be willing to make it worth your while. Seriously, you should at least hear him out."

I thought for a moment, and my mischievous side kicked in. James Hendrix was every bit as stingy as his old man. They didn't spend a penny that didn't absolutely have to be spent. Of course, I'd appreciated the training, knowing I'd eventually be doing my own projects, but that didn't mean I couldn't have a little fun.

"Okay, tell him I'll meet him, but he has to have the meeting at Morton's Steakhouse."

"Damn, you're trying to get me fired," Oren said, but I could hear the humor in his voice. "Okay, I'll tell him, but this isn't going to be good for me."

"Oh, but it's a lot of fun for me."

"Ugh, you're evil, boss, um, I mean, former boss, Xander," he stuttered, and I laughed again.

"Let me know what he says, Oren. You've got my number."

"Yeah, I will. Thanks, Xander, I appreciate it."

I hung up, not expecting to hear from them again. The guy wouldn't likely want to spend the hundred-plus dollars to feed me a fancy dinner just to talk me into coming back and being a whipping boy. I'd loved my job, I really had, but Leon made things tough, even for me. I'd worked hard for them, he'd said as much time and time again over the years, but since I left, it'd been radio silence.

I climbed into my truck and drove to Mom's. I'd just pulled into her driveway when Oren called, reminding me of other times I'd almost gotten home and been called out to go chase my fucking tail for that company.

"Ugh, I really don't want to relive this," I said to my steering wheel. I answered just to hear what he had to say.

"Hello?"

"Xander, he said yes and wants to meet tonight. Is that too soon?"

I considered saying no, but I didn't have plans. Rhys was busy with Brandon and Cliff for the rest of the week, so I was footloose and fancy-free—another thing my mom said.

"Yeah, I guess. What time?"

"Five is best if you can make it."

"Yeah, I'll be at Morton's Steakhouse at five. Oh, make sure he understands I'm not paying, even if I say no to whatever he's asking."

"No problem, I'll let him know. Xander, I… well, it'll be nice to see you," he said; then he quickly hung up.

Oren was a sweet guy and also tough, smart, and quick to get things done.

At one time I thought he might have a bit of a crush on me, but I was his boss and he was too old for me. Well, not really. If I liked older guys, he'd have been perfect. Then my mind immediately went to Rhys, the guy who was totally my type.

The smile was involuntary. I was all in for Rhys Healy, and he was into me. Life was great. At least, it would be if I could get the stupid council to stop being assholes.

I dashed into the house, hugged Mom, and told her what was going on.

"Wow, do you think they're going to offer you your job back?" she asked, looking concerned.

"Yeah, and I might take them up on it, at least temporarily. Mom, the council isn't going to approve my plan, not without me putting legal pressure on them. Then they'll make my life a living hell with inspections and crap like that. They'll delay me out of business."

Her eyes narrowed. "We've needed to replace that bunch for a while. You know, that's why I'm running for commissioner. I'm tired of them being clueless. We have to grow or we're going to die. There's no reason for it. Wilcox is sitting in a perfect spot with a great many assets. If we had the right people in place... well, we will get the right people in place."

She kissed my cheek, then disappeared into her office. I had been dismissed again in a way only my mother could do. Once she had a project in mind, there was no stopping her. The town council was, on average, seventy-five years old.

Even if the bridge issue hadn't happened, I'd been gone too long. I was seen as an outsider. That was the real issue.

Even though I was headed to a huge meal in Portland, I was hungry, so I fixed myself a ham and cheese sandwich, waved at Mom on my way out, and headed back to my old life. We'd just have to see where things led.

Rhys

I SAT ACROSS from Dad and Lucy as they signed the papers to transfer the hardware store to them. Stewie sat on the other side of me, smiling sadly. "Kids, this is a big deal for me. Been a long time coming, though."

Lucy reached over and took his hand. "We promise to treat it right," she said.

"Oh, I know you will. If I didn't know that already, I wouldn't have... well, it just feels right that it's going to your family."

He reached down into the ancient briefcase he'd brought with him and put a book on the table. "I'm getting married. No one will be surprised that I loved your aunt Helen. I begged her to marry me for more than twenty-five years, and she turned me down every time."

He stared at the book for a moment, and his serious expression stopped us from congratulating him. "I wasn't sure I should give this to you, but it shouldn't be with me. It, well, belongs to you, Helen's family. Right before she died, she gave me this and told me I should move on. Not that she hadn't said that to me a hundred times, mind you, but I'm as stubborn as she was. I held on to hope. She wanted me to understand why she hadn't accepted my proposal and said I had a right to know. I'm not sure I did, but now that I do, I agree, and it is time for me to move on. I've been dating a nice lady from Roseburg for several months now. I asked her to marry me last night, and she said yes."

"Congratulations, Stewie," I said, and he smiled.

"Yeah, son, thanks." He scooted the book to me. "This was private stuff, I think... I believe if she hadn't died right after giving me that, she would've taken it back and you'd have likely found it when you went through her things. Giving it back, well, it's like me letting Helen go. Take what you read with the knowledge your aunt loved fiercely. Even me, in her own way. I know that now. Just she couldn't love me the way I always hoped."

He drew in a deep breath and slowly let it go. I saw his spirit lift as the air left him. "I'll be at work tomorrow morning." He winked at Dad. Then he stood and smiled. "Boss," he added.

Dad laughed and stood as well. He hugged Stewie and shook his hand, like an opposite bro hug. "See you tomorrow, Stewie, and for real, congratulations. We will all want to meet the lucky lady."

"Oh, you will. My Sarah, she's one to be all in my business. After spending so many years alone, I'm strangely looking forward to that."

I chuckled. Aunt Helen might not have been his wife or even girlfriend, evidently, but she was still one to control her environment. Stewie clearly had a thing for strong women.

I wanted to have Dad's old crew begin deconstruction of the barn, so I had to get over to Brandon and Cliff's to complete the planning. But I'd ridden with Dad and Lucy, because I wanted to celebrate their purchase of the old hardware store—a new beginning for all of us. Brandon and Cliff's project could wait for now.

I flipped open the journal and began to read. At first I was confused. This wasn't Aunt Helen's journal. It was written by another person—a woman. But as I read on, it became clear.

My dearest, I know I can't tell you in person, so I will write it here in my private journal.

I don't understand where my love and passion for you comes from. We are both from this tiny nothing of a town. Like you've said, our family roots are so deeply set in the soil that you can't tear yourself away.

Tonight when we argued and you told me you would never leave Wilcox, I gave up hope. We can't be together here, Helen. The town, our families, would tear us apart. I know you think the world has changed, but the way the country passes laws, even changing state constitutions, tells me it's not changed that much.

I want you. I hunger for you as I have never hungered for anything ever. I have spent the past twenty years dreaming of the day when you and I can lie in each other's arms and stare at the stars.

I've dreamed of the mornings when I can wake up in your arms and not have to rush away to satisfy some family drama. That can be had in Portland or Seattle; I know it can. I truly will never understand why you refuse to go with me.

Helen, my beloved, even now I can't stem the tears. You've made your decision, and I must accept it.

Wilfred Crook asked me to marry him, and I've decided to say yes. I believe this is the best decision. It gets me out of Wilcox and away from you. Maybe with time I will learn to love him. Maybe in time I will stop burning so passionately for you.

I know I'm bitter, but as I write this, I hope your Healy roots were worth throwing me aside. I don't believe I will ever be able to forgive you for choosing that over me, but maybe you never loved me as much as I did you.

I go now to start the next chapter of my life, but even as bitter as I feel, I know, my sweet Helen, I will never forget you.

May the life you've chosen be worth it.

With all my broken heart,
Greta

"Dad," I asked, interrupting his and Lucy's conversation. "Who was Greta?"

Dad thought about it. "Haven't heard that name in a long time, but when I was young, living with Aunt Helen, she had a really close friend named Greta. Poor woman married a jackass and left town. She came back a few years later but ended up passing away. Broke your aunt's heart. Why?"

"Oh," I said as we pulled into the driveway.

"Here, you'll want to read this." I handed him the journal.

He opened it to the page where the gut-wrenching letter had been written.

Lucy watched, confused, as Dad read it and then whistled. "Damn, well, she kept that hidden."

He handed the journal to Lucy, who read it as well.

"Dad, that's so sad."

He nodded. "I always wondered why she never dated or married. Aunt Helen was a looker. Independent as could be, but she adored family, and, well, it just seemed so odd she didn't have her own."

"Do you think she loved her?"

Dad shrugged. "Hard to say."

"Oh, I love a good love story," Lucy said. "I know you two will be busy with the store. If you give me permission, I'll chase down more information about this Greta. She had to have meant something to Helen, or she wouldn't have given the journal to Stewie."

"Or she was just telling him she was a lesbian," I said.

"No," Dad remarked, "Lucy's right. She could've told him that any time. She showed him this because she had feelings for Greta. It was more than her sexual preference. I think she was showing him that she'd been in love."

"I'll dig," Lucy said as she climbed out of the car.

She was doing better. Her first treatment here in town was scheduled for tomorrow, and Dad had already warned me she was going to be sick and asked if I could help with the girls in case Lucy needed him full-time.

I was looking forward to what Lucy dug up. It hadn't occurred to me my aunt was gay. I'm not sure why, but it made perfect sense. I guess Stewie had somehow settled in my mind as her significant other. It just goes to show people's lives are complex and complicated. Making assumptions was seldom helpful.

I texted Xander then.

Me: *Good news, the hardware store is ours!*

Him: *That's awesome. Hopefully, we'll be able to keep you in business soon.*

Me: *LOL Hopefully. Can you meet me for a quick lunch before I head over to B and C's?*

Him: *No, on my way to Portland, will tell you details later.*

Me: *Cool, is it weird if I text Love you?*

Him: *LOL Oh no, not weird at all. Love you too. I'll call later.*

I was in love with Xander Petterson. Poor Aunt Helen, I wondered if she'd been in love with Greta for real. It hurt my heart to think of hers being broken. Even if she hadn't gone with Greta. I wondered what the whole story was, and I wished she was still around to fill us in.

At least I didn't face the same issues. The world had changed, I could love Xander in the open, and no one seemed to care. I lived in a small town, and I'm sure there was enough gossip to fill a stadium, but no more about us than there would be for any new couple.

The thought of choosing between my love for him and my hometown? "Aunt Helen, I'm so sorry," I said out loud.

BRANDON AND Cliff's project was going fine. They'd approved Johney's final blueprint and swore they wouldn't make many changes, which I knew they'd break because everyone does. But hopefully not too many changes.

If my plans were right, we'd begin work soon and have the foundation and framing up before the winter rains. If I were really lucky, we'd get the roof on too. There was a lot of work between now and then, but I was nothing if not persistent.

Now that Dad was managing the store, I would have plenty of time to dedicate to the project, which gave me hope that I could push forward at a reasonable speed.

Of course, I hoped Xander's project would be approved too. That way we could begin demolishing his home and set the foundation before the winter weather hit. I wasn't too optimistic, but one could hope.

Xander

I STARED AT the piece of paper in front of me, looked up at my former assistant, and back at the paper. "Is this real? It's a joke, isn't it?"

Oren shook his head, his bugging eyes telling me he was as surprised as I was at the amount James Hendrix had offered. "Why so much?" I asked. "If I was this valuable, why didn't they come after me?"

Oren shrugged. "I don't know, Xander, but I've been working for Mr. Hendrix since you left. He hasn't offered anyone this much even when he's gone after people Leon fired or made quit."

I stared at the number for a while longer. It was double what I had been making. Double, and I was making a lot before. It just blew my mind. "So, will you take it?" Oren asked.

I felt the heaviness of the entire sixteen-ounce steak I'd eaten at James's expense. "I need to think about it." By think, I meant talk to Rhys and Mom. I should take it. I shouldn't hesitate, and a few weeks ago, I wouldn't have. But now I had a guy I liked more than a huge paycheck. "Okay, well, um, I'll let you know, Oren, and thanks for, you know, putting this in front of me."

"Not me, dude. I make less than a quarter of that. This is all the Hendrix men. And if I'm honest, they aren't wrong to ask you back or pay you what you're worth. We've been hemorrhaging money since you left. Leon didn't want to admit it, but you were carrying the weight. Still, it wasn't until he… well, I probably shouldn't tell you this, but since you left because of him, I'll tell you, Leon cussed out James. That was the last straw."

I shook my head. "Leon was just a bunch of hot air. He never bothered me, not until he was going to force me to work the day I requested off weeks before. No, he didn't respect anyone—not me, not anyone, but… I enjoyed working for Hendrix."

"And now you can again and get paid what you're worth."

I cocked an eyebrow toward Oren. "Dude, how much will you get if I sign again?"

Oren laughed. "Am I that transparent?"

I chuckled. "Yes, but only to me. I've worked with you long enough to know your tells. Give me a moment, Oren. I need to make sure it works. If it does, you'll be the first to know."

Oren shook my hand, then led us out the door. I loved eating at Morton's, but when James put the proposed salary in front of me, I almost choked on the last bite of sour-cream baked potato.

Still, if I took the job, I'd bring Rhys here to celebrate.

I decided not to call him on the way home. I wanted to talk to him in person. He had responsibilities right now that I knew would keep him from coming to Portland with me. But we could work it out if I took it.

I thought about my project and my hope for redoing the Wilcox commercial properties. The universe was telling me that wouldn't happen, and the thought broke my heart. I'd been thinking about my Wilcox dreams since my days at Hendrix.

It was my own fault. I should've known that painting the bridges would piss off the wrong people. Hell, I knew they all had egos to match any mountain in Oregon, including our volcanos.... Oh well, live and learn.

I pulled up to my ugly home. I'd already signed the contract for the little house across from Rhys. I would still buy that one and let Mom find a tenant for it.

I forced my brain not to make decisions without fully thinking things through. Yet, if there was no work for me here—

"No, stop," I said to the inside of my vehicle and got out.

I needed time, and that's what I was going to give myself, even if I had to force myself to think about puppies or something.

Then my mind went to Rhys and me sliding together in his hot tub and I knew exactly how to distract myself.

Too bad the man in question wasn't available tonight. That would've been even better.

Rhys

"I KNOW, IT'S not great timing," Xander said, and I was having a hard time not pouting.

"So, if you take the job, what does that mean for your project?" I asked.

Xander shrugged. "If they agree, we can go forward, but you'll be in charge. But Rhys, unless I'm willing to fight the council in court, I'm guessing they won't approve it."

I sighed and shook my head. "Xander, it's a lot, but I can't blame you for taking it. It's a great opportunity, and the money sounds good."

"And," he added, "it's not that far from here to Portland. Maybe you can slip away some and hang out with me."

I chuckled. "I'm sure I will. I'm going to miss you, though. A lot."

Xander pulled me into an embrace, then kissed the soft spot under my ear—the spot that always made me putty in his hands.

We didn't have sex, probably because the news was so intense. We'd only just begun this thing together, but as Xander said, Portland wasn't that far—three hours at worst, and then only if there was rush hour traffic through the cities along Interstate 5.

I cuddled back into his arms. It was amazing to be there, but I wouldn't be getting this as much now he was going to be working out of town again.

I fell asleep thinking about that and had nightmares as a result. I couldn't remember all of them, but at one point, I was standing on a huge mountain and could see Xander but couldn't get down to him.

The next morning I kissed him, told him I supported any decision he made, and that I'd take every opportunity to spend time with him in Portland if he took the job.

I could tell that's what he was waiting for and knew from his expression that he would take the job. Not that I could blame him. The pay was excellent. And just from the times he talked about the projects he oversaw there, I knew he loved that kind of work.

I drove out to Brandon and Cliff's and was pleased to find the crew had already begun to disassemble the barn. They were piling the delicate barnwood onto pallets exactly as I'd instructed. Maybe that was a good sign.

I went to where the wood was being piled and was pleased to see that most of it was salvageable.

I went inside to look at the poles, and again, I was pleased they'd survived as well as they had. We were just lucky that Xander's relative—I couldn't remember the woman's name—had a new roof put on before she moved up north.

It was then it struck me who his aunt was. "Fuck me," I said out loud, and the guys who were standing next to me looked concerned.

I waved them off. "Was Xander's aunt my aunt's lover? Could it be that much of a coincidence?" I mumbled to myself. Surely not.

I shook it out of my head and continued to survey the work. "Hey, guys, I'm going to run into town," I announced, mostly so my head crewman could hear me. "I'll be back after lunch, and if you've got the siding off, we can tackle these beams."

My lead contractor nodded, and I didn't see Brandon or Cliff, so I climbed into my truck and headed to the hardware store to do my shift. Luckily, the work at the barn site was going well enough that I didn't need to micromanage and I could keep up my job there.

The store was a new venture for Dad. He'd been a construction guy for years, but there was a huge difference between doing construction and running a hardware store. Lucy had experience in retail, but her health came and went. She had a treatment every week, and she tended to get sick afterward, so it'd be good if I could continue to help out until Dad got his feet under him.

I walked into the store and felt my heart leap when I saw Xander helping a customer move a bag of dog food up to the counter. That reminded me that we needed to order some of those flat carts. I'd meant to talk to Stewie about that before he sold to Dad, but now I had more freedom to do what was necessary without getting his approval.

"Hey," Xander said as I walked over.

"Hey yourself." I kissed him chastely. "You got recruited to help, I see."

Xander chuckled. "Your dad is an expert at pulling in volunteers."

"You have no idea." I laughed.

"Come on back. I need to reorganize the canning room and check inventory."

"I've already done that," Stewie said from the front counter.

"Cool. Thanks, Stewie. What about the feed room?"

"Your dad got that yesterday afternoon. You got a shipment of the tack you ordered that needs to be priced and hung."

"Perfect, thanks," I said, and I led Xander to that side of the store.

"So, have you decided?" I asked as I opened a box and began to price the new horse reins.

Xander bit his bottom lip, but he nodded. "Yeah, I'm going to take it, at least temporarily. I've already decided I'll tell them it might only be for a short time, but it's like you said this morning—a good opportunity."

I kissed him, then bumped my head against his. "I'm glad for you, baby. I'm going to miss you bad, though."

"Yeah, about that—"

I cocked an eyebrow. "I gave up my apartment when I was let go before. There's a hotel close by the headquarters that takes corporate clients. It even has a small kitchenette. I was hoping we could create a schedule for you to come, you know, visit regularly?"

I laughed. "Conjugal visits?"

"Oh yeah," Xander whispered. "Very, very conjugal."

"Hey, you two, do your lovey stuff on your own time," Dad said as he came around the corner.

I rolled my eyes but laughed. "Yeah, whatever, Dad."

"Xander, Rhys says you might have a job in Portland. Going back to your old job?" Dad asked.

Xander nodded. "Yeah, I think I just decided to take it, especially with the project I had planned here not going so well."

"Oh, son, that's not unusual in these small towns. Just give them time. They almost always come around."

Xander nodded but didn't comment. "Oh, hey, I had a question. What was your aunt's name, the one who owned Brandon and Cliff's barn?"

"Aunt Greta?" he said, and I froze.

"Shit, it is her. Um, I have something to show you. Can you come by the house after I leave here?"

Xander looked confused but nodded. "Sure. Meanwhile, Mark, did you still need my help?"

"Oh, yeah, I almost forgot."

Dad and Xander left and went toward the back, where the new retail space would be.

I couldn't believe Xander's aunt was the one who'd written the journal about Aunt Helen. It was strange that I was in love with her nephew. It was like the world had come full circle.

I wasn't sure how I felt about showing the journal to Xander. I was sure the heart-wrenching letter was going to be hard for him to read, but it was his aunt's journal. He and his family should have it, not us. But I'd have to discuss that with Dad, since technically, Stewie had given it to both of us, and Lucy still had it.

I finished putting the new merchandise up, broke the boxes down, and put them in the back to be sent to recycling. Then I texted Lucy to let her know I'd need the journal. She texted me back immediately to say the journal was in their bedroom on the dresser. I knew she'd put it there to keep it out of the hands of my creative sisters. The journal still had empty pages, and to them, that was an invitation to draw pictures.

By the time I'd restocked the candy and soda up front, I just had time to find Xander, head back to the house, and get to the job site.

Xander followed me to the house, and I went in, happy to see it was empty. Lucy must have been at the store or shopping. I didn't know, but I wanted privacy for what I needed to do.

"Hey, can you sit in the living room? I've got something you need to see."

Xander did as I asked. I got the journal and brought it back to the living room.

"I just put two and two together this morning. I think this belonged to your aunt Greta."

When Xander saw the journal, his eyes grew bigger. "I thought maybe she destroyed this. When you didn't mention it before—"

"Wait, you know what this is?"

Xander nodded. "Yeah, sorry, Rhys, it was so personal. I didn't want to bring it up, but I'm the one who gave this to your aunt."

I stared at him, unsure of the feelings coursing through me. "You know your aunt was in love with mine?"

He nodded. "Yeah, we found this while tearing down my aunt's old house. It'd been hidden under the porch. Your aunt Helen was devastated and overcome with emotions when I gave it to her."

"I'm sure. Did you read it? The letter Greta wrote to her?"

Xander nodded. "Yeah, it was tough."

I stared at the journal for a few moments, then sighed. "Xander, it was gut-wrenching. I… what did my aunt say when you gave it to her?"

He shook his head and pondered a moment. I could tell he was struggling to tell me.

He took a deep breath and let it go. "Your aunt said she loved mine. Times were different then. She said she knew she'd made a mistake by not going but that she'd been afraid. She regretted not going with her."

I swallowed hard, unsure what to say. "I wish I'd known."

Xander drew me into a hug, the journal between us, and for just a moment, it felt like we were hugging her.

"You know now," Xander whispered.

"Yeah, we know now."

Xander

"WHY DIDN'T you tell me?" Rhys asked after we sat holding each other for several minutes.

"I don't out people, Rhys. Even those who've passed on. Your aunt's sexual identity should be her own. I'm sorry. I didn't mean to upset you."

"No, don't apologize. You're right, and I respect your decision. It's just, you know, overwhelming to learn all this."

"Yeah, I get it. I feel her here, you know, your aunt."

Rhys chuckled. "I think she's been here since before I started working on the place. It's comforting to know she's still around. I know that's crazy, but—"

"No," I said, "it's not crazy. I liked her, and it feels good that she's still here, still supporting you and your family."

"I sorta wish she'd reconnected with Greta, though, now that I think about it."

I cringed. "Yeah, that would be a nice thought. I've never felt my aunt's presence after her death. Her life was hard, especially in the end. I figured she was ready to go after all she'd been through. That's partly why I'm so happy Brandon and Cliff have taken over her old place and they're turning it into a beautiful home again. One filled with love."

"Oh, I think they will too. We got the siding down this morning. You should come and watch us take down the timbers. I think we'll have it dismantled by this evening. Tomorrow morning at the worst."

I chuckled. "I need to call my assistant and tell him I'm taking the job. Then I need to go celebrate, but maybe we can do that tonight," I said, waggling my eyebrows.

Rhys laughed. "Okay." He kissed me. "I've got ham and cheese. Want a quick sandwich before I have to head over?"

I nodded and sat at the counter while Rhys fixed us lunch. We chatted about the barn project, but Helen and Aunt Greta weighed heavily on us. It was sad to think they'd loved each other and lost it because of the times and Helen not being brave enough to go for what she wanted.

I knew it was more than that. Relationships are complicated when they're working out. Worse when they aren't.

When Rhys left, I sat in my truck, pulled my phone out, and called Oren.

"Hey, Xander. How are you?"

"Good, Oren, I'm going to take the job."

I had to pull the phone away from my ear when he yelled into the receiver.

"Oh, man," he said as he came back on the line. "That's great news. Okay, I've got all the paperwork ready. Want me to email it to you?"

I chuckled. Of course Oren would be prepared. "Yeah, man, send it over. I'll look at it this afternoon. When is James wanting me in?"

"Last week," he said, and I laughed.

"Okay, I'll make arrangements and get to Portland as soon as possible. If you've got a rundown on the jobs that need to be worked out, that'll be helpful. It's useful to be prepared before I step into that lion's den."

"Oh yeah, I just sent James a progress report. I can forward that to you with the paperwork."

"Cool, and Oren?"

"Yeah?" he replied.

"Glad to be working with you again."

I could almost hear the guy blush. He was a fantastic employee, the best and most organized I'd ever met.

"It's my pleasure too, Xander. See you soon, okay?"

"Yeah, buddy, see you soon."

I hung up feeling good, like it was meant to be. As I drove toward Aunt Greta's old farm, it felt like putting the journal in the hands of Helen's family was the right thing too. The fact that Helen had given the journal to Stewie was confusing and intriguing until Rhys told me the story of Stewie getting married and giving the journal back as a way to let go of his dreams and hopes around Helen.

It was like a tragic love story. I guess that's exactly what it was. Sad, no matter how you looked at it. Thank goodness the world had changed, right?

It was jarring to see the barn without the siding. It had been a part of my childhood. I'd had my first kiss there—with Brandon, of course, even if it wasn't anywhere near as good as I'd hoped. Poor Brandon and I were not made for one another.

Of course, now he had Cliff, and that relationship was beautiful. I had amazing and talented Rhys. I thought of his incredible tongue and smiled. Very talented.

I backed my truck up, sat on the tailgate, and watched as they took the structure down. I'd told Rhys I hadn't felt my aunt, but it was almost like she was with me now.

I knew that was just me being sentimental. I didn't even know if she cared about the old barn.

The house was where she'd been born and where her last good memories were. I know I had good memories there… mixed memories. That's what was there for me, my mom, and probably her—a lot of mixed memories.

I ended up leaving before Rhys's crew finished. I kissed Rhys and told him I'd see him tonight for that celebratory dinner and dessert. I was especially looking forward to the dessert.

Then I stopped by the grocery store and grabbed a frozen lasagna and a bottle of wine. I didn't cook, but the Stouffer's was almost as good as Mom made, not that I'd ever tell her that.

I popped the lasagna into the oven when I got home, opened the bottle of wine to let it breathe, and went to shower. I wanted to be clean and ready for tonight. If I had to be away from Rhys, I was going to enjoy every moment he and I had together.

I wasn't going to let life get in the way of my relationship with Rhys like it had Helen and Aunt Greta. No fucking way. Life was too short, and regret wasn't something I cared to live with. I loved my handsome Rhys and would do what I could to make our relationship work.

Rhys

"UGH, XANDER, really? You have to work this weekend?"

"Yeah, I know it sucks. They're so screwed, having fired Leon, my predecessor. Can you come up?"

"No, sorry. Lucy's sick from her last treatment, and Dad has to work at the store. I've got kid duty."

"Damn," Xander said, and we sighed simultaneously. "Life is getting in the way."

"Yeah, it does that, but if Lucy feels better during the week, I'll try to get up there, or maybe you can beg off a day or two," I said, hoping to make us both feel better.

"How's the barn project going?" Xander asked.

"Great, we got the foundation poured, and it's setting. Hope to start framing next week."

"Dang, you're moving along. Wish I could be there to see your progress."

I didn't respond. There wasn't much to say. I wanted him here every hour of every damned day. I missed him all the fucking time, but it didn't do either of us any good to say that. I didn't want him to feel bad.

"Oh, did you hear back from the council?" I asked.

"No. I asked Jason and Tim to reach out and ask, but I'm guessing they're figuring out how to turn me down without it becoming an issue."

"They're assholes. On a positive note, I saw three people running for council to replace them, including the mayor. That's good, right?"

Xander laughed. "Oh yeah. My mom is behind a lot of that. She's pretty mad about the way they're acting. Not just about me. They turned down at least two major projects that would've helped Wilcox economically. The town is pretty pissed off about those too."

"Do you think these new folks will win?"

"No idea. Politics isn't my game. She's feeling good about it, though. Won't stop talking about it."

I laughed. Ellen was a lot, to say the least. "It's been a long time since I've been around Ms. Polly, Tim's wife. I'm guessing she'd be an amazing mayor. Tough but fair."

"She's Mom's best friend," Xander said, and I could hear the affection in his voice.

"Yeah, she used to hang out here when I lived with Aunt Helen. They were peas in a pod. She'd be an amazing mayor—better than the jackwad there now."

Xander laughed again. "Well, I mean, he's a pretty good guy usually. I remember him growing up. He'd come over to the house frequently when Dad was still alive, but lately, he's been a bit of a jerk."

Just then the girls burst through the front door, creating havoc. "Hey, babe, I have to go. The girls just got home."

"Yeah, I heard. Love you, Rhys," he said.

"I love you too," I said just as Chelsie spilled a juice box on the floor. One look at Lucy and I knew I needed to take over. "Bye," I quickly said and hung up.

"Hey, why don't you go take a break while I skin this little monster right here," I said to Lucy as I scooped my sister up and began to tickle her.

"Hey, no fair," she yelled, but she laughed when I put her down.

"Okay, go get a paper towel and wipe this mess up. Jenny, up to your bedroom and start your homework. No arguing. I bought pizza, and I'll eat every bite if you say one word."

She stuck her tongue out at me but dashed upstairs.

"You bought pizza again?" Lucy asked, and I could tell she was struggling to stay upright.

I went over, linked my arm through hers, and escorted her to the sofa. "My house, my rules," I whispered, and Lucy laughed and pinched my arm.

"I promise to make broccoli-something tomorrow, but tonight is definitely a pizza night. What do you want on yours? I was just about to order."

"Sounded to me like you were talking sweet nothings with your man," she said as she lay back on the sofa.

I chuckled. "You are too observant but not wrong." I plopped down on the loveseat opposite her. "I miss him something crazy. I know that's ridiculous."

"Nonsense. It'd be ridiculous if you didn't feel that way. Xander is one hot puppy," she replied, and I choked.

"Did you just call my guy hot?"

"Oh yeah, anyone with eyes would," she said. "I'm going to take a little nap. Is that okay?" she asked, and I could tell she was already drifting off.

I got up, and despite the humidity in the house, I grabbed the blanket and covered her. She pulled the covers up under her chin. I hated seeing how hard the treatments were on her. It seemed like lately they were making her sicker and sicker. Hopefully that was a sign the chemo was working. God, please let the chemo be working.

I inspected the cleanup, and feeling she'd done her best, I kissed the top of Chelsie's head and sent her up the stairs to start her homework.

Then I grabbed my WetJet and finished the job, making sure to get up all the sticky. I called in the pizza, and even though Lucy hadn't replied, I knew her favorite—Canadian bacon, black olives, mushrooms, and extra sauce.

Our pizza place was super slow, but Dad would be home in about an hour, which should be perfect timing. I told the restaurant that Dad would be by to pick it up. Of course, it was so routine now that I didn't even have to say it. Everything had become routine since I moved back home.

I loved it. I liked knowing that the pizza place knew me by name and that Dad would pick it up in an hour. I loved that I knew almost everyone I met on the street as I walked to work.

I loved that I liked Ellen, Xander's mom, and I loved that I knew the people she had recruited to run for city council. I liked almost everything about my small town, except—and this was a fucking big except—I missed Xander. It felt wrong that he wasn't here.

Secretly I hoped Ellen got her way and the dinosaurs on the council were replaced and got out of Xander's way. Then maybe he'd come home and I'd have him here with me again. Things would be perfect.

I glanced at where Lucy lay sleeping on the sofa and thought, mostly perfect. If she got better, that would be perfect. She and Dad could move into a home of their own. Then Xander and I could move here and live our best lives. That's what I really wanted. I wanted what we'd had for a brief moment before it was swept away.

I needed to check on my crew, but decided to do that tomorrow morning. If there were any problems, they'd have called me. Luckily all the guys were super qualified and experienced.

Almost any of them could've run the project without me. Dad had known the guys most of his adult life, even when I was a kid.

I was frustrated that Xander's project hadn't been approved. With that crew, we could divide and conquer those builds quickly, putting the men as individual house project managers.

I forced myself not to get upset and to concentrate on the tasks at hand. I wandered upstairs and had to break up an argument between the girls over something I didn't understand. Once they were refocused on their homework, I went down to my area and began to clean up.

I'd been so busy lately I'd let my personal space get dirty, which wasn't something I could stand for long. I liked it clean. I'd need to find time to mop the floors and dust, but for now, I'd be happy just getting my laundry done. There didn't seem to be enough hours in the day any longer.

Of course, managing my sisters made that more difficult, and I don't think Dad or Lucy had anticipated all the work the hardware store would bring them. But Dad seemed to be loving it.

The girls' birthday was next on the agenda. Summer school ended next week, then we'd have their birthday, and the regular school year would begin. All of it was spinning so fast.

I collapsed on my bed, closed my eyes, and thought about Xander. *God, I miss him*, I thought as I drifted off to sleep. When Jenny tapped my forehead to wake me, I chuckled. "I think I fell asleep."

She laughed, and I glanced up to see both her and Chelsie. "Did you two get done with your homework?" They both nodded. "Wait, why are you standing here? What've you done?" I asked, suspicious all of a sudden.

Chelsie rolled her eyes and handed me a picture they'd drawn and colored. It was clearly me and Xander. I could tell by the hat they'd drawn for Xander, and of course, they always drew me the same way.

Over our shoulders was an angel, and I instantly knew who it was. "Who's this?" I asked, just to have them tell me.

"Aunt Helen. She's sad you and Xander aren't together."

I gasped, then swallowed my surprise. "She is? How do you know?" I asked.

"Because she was in our dream," Jenny said as Chelsie handed me the drawing. Then they left me in shocked silence.

I stared at the picture and shook my head. "Okay, Aunt Helen, this is getting a little weird," I said, and for a moment, I could've sworn I heard her laugh.

Xander

I THOUGHT I'D worked my butt off before, but with Leon gone, I was working both his and my jobs. I knew they were paying me twice what I'd made before, but that didn't mean I'd agreed to do twice the work.

Some extra duties made sense, but it was too much. As it was, I worked seven days a week, often from sunup to sundown. Finally, after getting off the phone with my boyfriend, who I hadn't seen in two fucking weeks, I'd had enough.

I used the walkie to tell Oren I was headed over to headquarters to talk to James. "Not sure when I'll be back."

"Got it, boss. Do you need me to send anything for your meeting?" Always the efficient one.

"No, not this time. Just hold down the fort."

"Got it," he replied. If it hadn't been for Oren, there's no way this would've worked. I knew for a fact he was putting in the same number of hours as I was. It needed to stop for him too.

I called Hendrix's secretary and told her I needed a moment with James, and she confirmed he was available. "Good, see you in a moment," I told her and drove over.

I was immediately shown back, which was one of the things I liked about the Hendrix corporation—how receptive James and his dad were to meeting their employees.

James looked up from his desk and nodded as I walked in. "Hello, Xander, what's up?"

"Work," I said, jumping right into it. "James, I've been working over ninety hours a week since I started. I haven't seen my family or my boyfriend in weeks. It's the same for my guys and Oren too."

James sat back and sighed. "Yeah, we appreciate how hard you all are working. Here, let me show you what's going on." He paused for a moment, opened his desk, pulled out a paper package, and handed it to me.

I looked over the package expecting to see some rush order. Instead, I found myself looking at a commitment to merge with Direct Construction—our largest competitor in the Pacific Northwest.

"Wow, okay, when did this come about?"

James looked at me over his glasses and nodded. "About a week before I offered you your job back. Their only requirement was that we fire Leon."

I was taken aback for a moment, then remembered an incident where Leon told Direct's CEO to fuck himself when they won a bid over us. "Oh, well, that makes sense," I said. "So that's why I got the big bonus for coming back."

James smiled. "Part of the reason. They asked about you during the negotiations too. I... well, I shouldn't have let you go. Leon was pissed and convinced us that you'd been lipping off to him. Of course, Oren was there and confirmed the only person lipping off was Leon."

"I... okay, so you don't want to hire someone to replace Leon because, when the merger happens, we'll absorb some of their employees?"

He nodded. "Yep, exactly. However, if you need me, I can step in. It's been a minute or so since I've managed a crew, but I can help."

"I hate to ask, but yeah, if we don't get some help, both Oren and I are going to crash and burn soon, and I'm going to throw away any chances I have at keeping my sweetheart."

James laughed. "We don't want that. Okay. I'll step in and give you a break. Can you fill me in on the details?"

Oren had just sent out a progress report, so I pulled it up on my phone, and knowing James had it too, I went over the details. "Okay, got it. I'll step in this weekend and field any calls. Then let's give Oren Monday and Tuesday off. Does that work?"

I stood up and took James's hand. "It works great, boss, and thanks. I can use forty-eight hours to get my head on straight again."

James winked at me and dismissed me like he always did. Once again, I was happy to have a boss I could depend on. No complaining about me making enough that I should be able to do the job by myself like some bosses would. He hadn't hesitated to step up.

I thought about texting Rhys and telling him the good news, but then decided I'd rather surprise him. I knew he was busy too, and I really needed the two days to crash. Sleep would be very helpful before I came back to face the beast again.

Now that I knew a merger was in my near future, I needed to be even more rested. Direct was a good company. They'd won as many contracts in the area as we had. The merger would be good but stressful, and I'm sure we didn't operate the same way.

That was something to stress over later. For now, I had the weekend and my super sexy man to keep my thoughts occupied. I definitely needed it.

Rhys

LUCY IMPROVED as the weekend drew nearer, for which I thanked God. I was thinking about slipping away and heading north to see Xander when one of the guys shot his damned hand with the nail gun. It wouldn't kill him, but it was an amateur move, and I'd need to step in and cover for him until he got better.

Not that I minded the work. I missed getting my hands dirty. I was already going to do the electrical work myself, with the help of Louis, who said he was thinking about getting his electrician license, but I would've liked to have had a few days with my guy. Oh well, it couldn't be helped.

We'd just lifted and set the last trusses on top of the barn reconstruction when I recognized the truck that pulled in front of Brandon and Cliff's construction trailer. If I hadn't been literally hanging off the side of a crane, I'd have embarrassed the crap out of myself by running over and jumping into Xander's arms. Unfortunately I had to stay put and finish nailing the truss into place.

The crane operator eventually lowered me, and I did what I wanted. I pulled my guy into a hug and kissed him square on the lips to applause from the crew. I flipped them off and led Xander away so we could talk.

"So, what's this about? Did you get fired?" I asked.

"Wow, you don't have a lot of faith in me, do ya?"

I laughed. "I have all the faith in you. Damn, I missed you so bad." I embraced him again and kissed him deeply this time, tongue and all.

When we pulled back, he moaned. "Okay, let's go home," he said as he pulled me caveman-style toward his truck.

"No, dude," I said, laughing. "I have to stay and help with the trusses. I want to get the roof on before Monday. The metal roofing company is coming on Tuesday to install."

"You kiss me like that, then leave me to suffer. You're a tease, Rhys Healy, a total tease."

I leaned over and gave him a peck. "Yeah, but I'll make it up to you later. How long can you stay?"

"They gave me the weekend off. I plan to eat, sleep, and fuck," he whispered. "If you'll let me."

"Oh yeah, I'll let you. I can't do the sleeping part much," I said, pointing at the building project behind me, "but there'll be plenty of time for the fucking."

Xander chuckled, then pulled away. "Are Brandon and Cliff home? I wanted to see them before I got out of your way."

"No, they're over at the Owens place—something to do with one of Cliff's tanks going wrong. I don't know. He's told me about his aquaponic project, but it's like listening to someone explain the Greek philosophies."

Xander nodded. "Yeah, he's into it. When will you be done? I'll have dinner ready."

"Really? You're going to cook?" I asked, my eyebrow rising.

"On no, that would suck for both of us and not in the way I want to suck for you," he said. "But I can go grab fried chicken at the grocery store. You like fried chicken, right?"

"Sure, that works for me." I looked at my watch. "I'd say six at the latest. If we can get to a good stopping point, I'll try to get done earlier."

"I'll hold you to that," he said, and I watched him leave for the Owens house across the street.

I wished I could've gone with him, but life seemed determined to get in our way.

I let the crane guy hoist me back up to help secure the trusses so we could hopefully get the plywood decking down tomorrow. If I was lucky, it'd all be done so we could spend Sunday doing his "sleep, eat, and fuck" idea.

I was exhausted when we were done that evening. One side of the plywood was on, so I could leave the rest for the guys to finish tomorrow. I drove home, cursing that I couldn't just crawl into my hot tub with Xander. Unfortunately, I knew that if I did, I'd end up with two just-turned-seven-year-olds wanting to hang out with Xander. They missed him almost as much as I did.

The thought was cute, but I was so not sharing him with anyone tonight.

I pulled into his driveway around five, and he walked out just in time for me to land in his arms. "Mmm, I've missed you so bad. You're all I could think about all day."

Xander smiled. "Did you get done?"

"No, but the guys said they can finish tomorrow… without me." I smiled up at him. "It appears I'm all yours."

He pushed me back without letting go and looked me over. "You look a little worse for wear. Come and get a shower. I'll run to the store and pick up supper. Anything you want besides the chicken?"

"Oh yeah, but nothing you'll have to buy," I said, and he laughed.

I climbed into his ugly-ass shower and was happy he had strong water pressure. It felt good to let it beat my tired muscles back into focus. By the time I dried off and slipped into the clean clothes I'd left here last time, I was ready to spend an evening with him.

After supper we cuddled on his huge couch and watched TV. I hadn't even realized I was asleep until Xander woke me. Then he picked me up like I weighed the same as the girls and hauled me to his bedroom.

I let him undress me and watched him as he did. Then he did a little striptease for me, and my cock stood to attention.

"Turn over. Massage first," he said. I kinda preferred sucking first, but I wasn't going to refuse a massage. I rolled over, and Xander pulled a bottle from his drawer. For a moment, I thought he was going to lube me up, and I wasn't going to complain if he did.

Instead he poured liquid into his hands, set the bottle down, and began to massage my tired muscles. "Oh fuck," I moaned. Xander hadn't done this for me before, but he had magic hands that matched perfectly with his magic dick.

I was just about to fall asleep when Xander reached under me, lifted my ass slightly, and began to rim me. Fully awake now, I leaned back against his tongue.

I moaned as he probed my sensitive flesh and then used his fingers to explore my hole, sending shockwaves of pleasure through my entire body.

When I got on all fours, I began to beg. "Xander, please, I need you inside me."

He chuckled and let the oil, now mixed with his saliva, act as a lubricant for his cock. He teased me, rubbing against my hole, knowing that made my brain short-circuit.

"Fuck…. God… fuck… Xander," I cried as he moved up and down, teasing me, prepping me for what I needed so much.

When he grabbed the lube, I whimpered, need coursing through me. His now-lubed head bumped against my hole, and I instantly pushed back, wanting him enough that I was willing to deal with the burn.

"Slow down," he whispered. "I'll do you right, Rhys. Let me give this to you."

The sweetness in his voice calmed me long enough for Xander to reposition himself and grab his cock. He used his head to rub up and down my hole, sending more electrical pulses through me.

I rocked back and forth as his head teased my opening. Then, when he finally pushed inside, I sucked in air and then forced myself to relax.

Xander filled me, and what must have been muscle memory from the glorious sex we'd had the past few months drew his cock deeper and deeper.

"Yeah, fuck. I need you, baby. Yeah," I exclaimed as his big stiff cock continued to stretch me. When he pulled out, I cried, "Fuck me, Xander, I need—"

I didn't get the words out before Xander slammed his cock deep inside me. My nerve endings exploded in pleasure, which caused me to sit up. Xander's strong arms wrapped around me and held me as his cock continued to drive into me.

"Fuck," I mumbled as he leaned down and took my mouth with his. I fucking loved when Xander took me like this—driving into me as he held me from behind. I never felt more loved.

My brain was scrambled as he continued to take me again and again.

Finally he asked me to lie down, and when I did, he lifted my legs to rest on his shoulders and stretched me as he leaned forward and pushed his cock back inside.

"I love you," he said when I glanced up at him, and he held that position, causing my heart to quake. I nodded, not able to speak for fear of becoming emotional. Then he spared me by fucking me with all he had.

"God, fuck," I yelled as he slammed into me again and again.

Xander was a sex god who knew how to manipulate my body so I could come when he demanded. When he directed his cock at my prostate, I wanted to protest—I didn't want our lovemaking to end—but then I saw stars as he plowed it again and again until I shot so hard my cum hit him in the face.

My entire body tingled when he smiled and licked the cum off his lips. He pulled out, began to jack off, and came within seconds.

Xander's eyes darkened as he leaned over and took my mouth, and we showed each other just how much we felt.

Xander

THE NEXT morning I got up and showered, surprised at how much energy I had, especially after working so many hours. Rhys was still sound asleep, so I got the coffee brewing, I kissed him awake, and then straddled him in bed.

"Hey, handsome," I said. He smiled but didn't open his eyes. "Don't you wanna wake up and go hiking with me?"

"Ugh, hiking? You mean lying around. I believe you promised me eating, sleeping, and fucking." He bucked up against me, and I laughed.

I lay on top of him and kissed his cute face. "We can eat, sleep, fuck, and go hiking."

"Start with the fucking," he said, and before I knew it, he'd flipped me. We made love again, and after coffee and a shower together, I dragged him to our local park and up the winding road that crossed into the mountains.

"It's so beautiful here," Rhys said. "I forgot all about this park."

I smiled and took his hand in mine as we wound our way up the mountainside to where I knew the view was spectacular. The river flowed from Wilcox into the coastal mountain range and finally into the ocean, and from here, you could see for miles as the river snaked its way along.

Rhys gasped when we came to the lookout. "You haven't been here before?" I asked.

He shook his head. "No, we only ever visited the lower area. Sometimes Aunt Helen brought a picnic. Apparently, one of my way-back uncles donated the land."

"Ha, that's funny. My second great-grandfather donated part of the park as well."

Rhys leaned into me when we sat on a boulder with the perfect view. "It's cool that our families have such a deep-rooted background here in this county," he said.

"Yeah, my mom and Aunt Greta used to tell me our family history every chance they got."

"Oh, same with Aunt Helen. 'Rhys,'" he mimicked, "'your ancestors were some of the first settlers here in Wilcox. They came both by wagon train and by ship.'"

I laughed at how much he sounded like his late aunt and how similar the stories were to mine. "Why do you think they couldn't work it out?" Rhys asked, and I immediately knew he was talking about Helen and Aunt Greta.

I shrugged. "I mean, it was very different back then. LGBTQ people weren't accepted in any way. I guess we're just lucky things have changed."

"Yeah, but it's… it's just sad."

I put my arm around him and drew him closer. "We don't know what was happening in their lives. Aunt Greta married a total jackass, and he made her life miserable. Your aunt Helen met and loved Stewie, even though they weren't lovers. Life isn't always easy, but even my aunt Greta did the best she could with what she had."

"Do you really believe that?" he asked.

"Yeah. I've always felt bad about my aunt's life. She struggled during the last part, but she was strong and resilient. Did I tell you she was the first person I came out to?" I asked, and Rhys smiled.

"That's funny. Aunt Helen was the first person I told."

"I think maybe somehow we knew they'd understand. That they were like us."

Rhys turned to stare out over the amazing vista. "Let's not make the same mistake they did, okay?" he asked.

I leaned down and kissed the top of his head. "Okay, we'll do better," I whispered.

We were quiet as we walked down the path back to the truck. We weren't far from Brandon and Cliff's, so we drove by. Rhys was pleased his guys had finished the roof and had already packed up and gone.

"You've done great with this," I said as I walked around the now framed and roofed structure.

"It's still got a long way to go, but we're ahead of schedule. Thanks," Rhys said.

"I almost regret selling it now. Not that I'd want Brandon to know that. He fell in love with this place long ago, long before I could see it as anything but the last place my aunt was happy."

"They're going to make it an amazing place to live. Besides, Brandon's your bestie. It's not like you won't be over here plenty."

He wasn't wrong. I hadn't spent as much time here as I used to, mostly because I'd been working like crazy for years. Also, Levi and Brandon had families, and I felt like the third wheel. I wondered if maybe now that I had Rhys, that'd be different.

When Rhys appeared pleased with the work, we returned to the truck and left. Brandon and Cliff were out of town or I would've talked Rhys into spending some quality time with them, but I'd promised sleep, eating, and fucking. We'd gotten a good start on the sleeping and fucking. Now I needed to feed my man.

"Mind going for a ride?" I asked.

Rhys shrugged, so I drove toward the mountains. We were forty-five minutes from the best steak house and dive restaurant. We held hands all the way, and I wished we had another forty-five minutes to spend together in my truck.

When the adorable little town appeared, I saw Rhys sit up. "What's this?" he asked.

"Millersville. It's an old lumber camp that never went away. It grew into this. You know the railroad that runs through town?" He nodded. "Well, this is where it leads. The timber company used to ship all the lumber from here to Wilcox. From there it was distributed to sawmills around Oregon. So we were a bit of a hub."

Rhys looked around and seemed intrigued by the town. When I pulled in front of an ancient-looking building that used to be an old gas station, Rhys cocked an eyebrow and looked at me. "For real?" he asked.

"Trust me. This is a 'don't judge a book by the cover' thing, like your bar in Eugene, remember?" I asked. "My dad's family is from this area. They were loggers back in the day. We used to come here when I was a kid. It hasn't changed hardly at all, which you'll be thankful for when you taste the food," I said as I led him to the front door.

The place was dark and a little dingy. We sat down, and a young man who introduced himself as Jake came and took our drinks order.

"What's good?" Rhys asked.

"Everything. If you want a steak, the sirloin is something from the heavens. We cook it to order, though, so it's at least a thirty-minute wait."

Rhys studied the menu and then smiled. "I love mac-n-cheese, and they have popper flavored. Is it good?" he asked, and I had to shrug. That was new. I'd never had it before.

Jake returned to get our order, and I asked, "What's up with the popper mac-n-cheese?"

Jake smiled. "I know it's new, but it's good. Trust me."

I lifted the beer he'd just dropped off and called, "Hear! Hear!" much to his delight.

"I'll have the popper mac-n-cheese," Rhys said.

"I'll have the porterhouse, medium, and a baked potato," I said, thinking I could share part of the ginormous steak with Rhys if he wanted more than the mac-n-cheese.

Jake left us, and I reached over and took Rhys's hand. "I have great memories here. I hope it's still as good," I whispered.

"In my experience, gay men have a way around the kitchen, so I wouldn't be too concerned," Rhys whispered back.

"What? You think Jake is family?"

Rhys just laughed. "Baby, if he swished any harder, he'd fall over. Besides, he was giving you the fuck-me look."

"Dude, he was not," I said, but I looked at the kitchen doors Jake had just disappeared through.

"Whatever, I'm telling you, I recognize that look 'cause I give it to you all the time," he said.

I picked up his hand and kissed it. "Never fear, I'm yours for as long as you want me."

"Well, that's something we should discuss, don't you think? Do you want to be exclusive with this? You're working in Portland, and I'm here, and there's a lot of space between us."

"Wait, do you want to see others? Be open?" I asked.

Rhys shrugged. "Listen, Xander, I don't have the most voracious libido, but I know others do… you might. I don't need to be exclusive to be happy as long as you save the heart stuff for me. I'm good either way."

"So," I lowered my voice again, "you're telling me you wouldn't mind me turning cute little Jake there over a table and having at it?"

Rhys leaned back. "If you have that itch and want to scratch it, scratch away, but maybe not when I'm sitting right here with you."

I thought about it for a moment. "I'm not as open-minded as you. I like the thought of exclusivity. I'm old-fashioned that way, I guess."

"Really?" Rhys asked, seeming genuinely surprised.

"Well, yeah, I mean, I didn't date much and only screwed around when it was absolutely necessary to prevent spontaneously combusting, but I like the thought of keeping myself just for you. That gives me something to look forward to when I come home."

"Okay, well, I won't be fucking around anyway, so if you want to make this a monogamous thing, I'm in."

Jake came around the table just as he said that, and his mouth dropped open. "Um, sorry. Um, here's your salad." He blushed and then dashed back into the kitchen.

Both Rhys and I laughed. "Poor guy. We must've scared him shitless."

"More like turned him on," Rhys said.

"Either way, thanks for the talk. I feel better knowing where we stand."

Rhys leaned over the table and kissed me, maybe a little too intensely for a public restaurant. Luckily we were the only people there besides poor Jake.

Rhys

THE DAY had been perfect. I think Xander and I needed it, especially considering how stressful our lives had been. I held him for too long Monday morning, my heart already yearning for him to be back, and he hadn't even left yet.

Alas, he had to leave, and I watched him go, even if it made me look pathetic. I didn't have any work pulling me to Brandon and Cliff's since the roofers wouldn't be there until tomorrow, so I went to the hardware store, planning to spend the day with them.

Dad had upped my pay, even though I hadn't asked him to, and with the money I was making from Brandon and Cliff's barn project, I was feeling pretty good about my bank account. Even when I was working for Dad in Portland, I didn't spend money like many friends my age. It wasn't like I was thrifty, but I hated shopping and I was busy.

Still, I seemed to know what people wanted to buy. Lucy was still doing well, so I sat down with her in the office, and we went over all the fun merchandise for the new retail space. We'd had Memorial Day and Fourth of July since we'd opened the space to the public, and the stock for both had all but sold out. The stuff we didn't sell would be knocked 50 percent off. So we had zero losses. It was definitely time to expand.

I sat with Lucy as she shared her thoughts. "I think I want to open a register back here," Lucy said.

"Do you think there'll be enough sales to support an extra cashier?" I asked.

Lucy shrugged. "Yeah, if the cashier is me," she added.

I turned to her, a little surprised she'd take this on. "Well, yeah, then I agree. You can always lock the door and force people to pay up front."

She nodded and pointed at a set of beautiful fairy sculptures. "I want to put this sort of stuff in here too. I want to call this the Seed Store like the old sign out front reads. If we stock garden items, that's a fun theme we can play on. If it does well, I can add more and more merchandise. What I don't want to do is bankrupt us with my fancy dreams of a fun retail space."

"It's hard not to get carried away. I struggle with that," I said.

After Lucy and I made our orders, we walked around and did inventory of each new section. Everything was selling well.

So far it seemed like my plan was working as, day by day, we got a little busier. I was afraid that when Dad bought Stewie out, it might cause some confusion and we'd lose customers, but many residents said they thought it was appropriate that Helen's kids, meaning Dad and me, had taken over.

By the time I was done with the day, I was tired. I jogged back to my house and stared sadly across the river to where I'd spent an amazing weekend with Xander. God, I missed him so much, but busy people, busy lives. His work ethic was one of the things I loved about him. That didn't mean I didn't want him here with me after a long day of work.

I kissed the tops of my sisters' heads when I walked into the house. I went over to the kitchen where Lucy was working and asked if I could help. "No, I got this," she said, smiling, so I bumped her shoulder in the way we did to show affection and told her I was going to jump in the hot tub and shower.

I lay back in the hot tub and let the jets work their magic. Again, I longed for Xander so much that I fell asleep thinking of him, and my mind drifted to the same dream where I was standing on a cliff far from Xander, unable to get to him.

My subconscious was considering the same thing I was. Were we too far apart? It might do me some good to figure that out ahead of time, because I would be devastated if we broke up. If things got even deeper, it might destroy me, just as sure as falling off the cliff in my dream.

Xander

MONDAY AND Tuesday were sheer hell. As much as I appreciated him, I didn't fully grasp what my assistant did for me until he wasn't there. By the time he returned to work on Wednesday, I could almost have kissed the man.

On Thursday my boss and his father asked Oren and me to meet the Direct Construction owners. Of course I'd already met them many times before. We ran in the same circles, considering we were competitors and often bid for the same jobs.

I sat across from James, his dad, and the two owners of Direct. I gave Oren a questioning glance, and he quickly returned a *no idea* shrug.

"Xander, Oren, as you know, we're merging with our competitor, Direct Construction. We believe we can be much more efficient if we work together. We'll be filling positions starting as soon as next month, but before we do, we wanted to offer each of you a promotion."

Old man Hendrix pushed two envelopes toward us, then gestured for us to open them. I opened mine and pulled out a letter of intent. My mouth dropped when I read "Vice President of Project Management."

I glanced at Oren, who was promoted to operations manager. No surprise, Oren could easily be the chief operations officer if it weren't going to one of the four men across the table.

"I accept," Oren said.

"I'll need a little more time, but this is a great honor. Just so we're clear, this is Leon's old position, correct?"

Both my bosses nodded, and I noticed the other two men scowl. They really disliked Leon, not that I could blame them.

"Yes, you'll be in charge of managing all the project managers. It also comes with a significant raise, which will be adequate, considering you'll manage both our current projects and the projects Direct brings with them."

"May I ask what those entail?" I asked and got a smile from James. Clearly, that was the right question.

I listened as they went through their current projects, which were a lot. I smiled. I'd love to take those on. I'd be helping to build everything from a fancy library and performance hall in Vancouver, Washington, to a series of large filling stations along the interstate. It was the kind of diversity I liked in my workload—much greater than I'd had working for Hendrix.

"I can let you know by the end of the week," I said as I stood to shake hands.

When we walked out, Oren hugged me. "I never thought we'd get promoted. This is a family company and all, but you know this is as high as you can go. Direct is run by father and son too. I mean, this is the top," Oren said again.

I patted him on the back and smiled at his enthusiasm. I had a lot to think about. I would be at the top of my game if I took the job. I'd be running projects up and down the Pacific Northwest. But then I thought of the project back home.

Wilcox didn't want me, I reminded myself. Considering how much trouble they'd given me over the houses, there was little chance I'd get to build on the commercial enterprises. This promotion and income were more than I could've dreamed of. I'd be a fool not to take it… or I'd be a fool to take it without talking to Rhys first.

Once James was back in his office, I knocked on his door and went in. "Hey, I know I took off the weekend, but I need to go talk to… well, my people before I agree to this."

"Yeah, I figured. Oren and I can cover for you. Go talk to your guy and see if you can persuade him into moving here. Oren says he has construction experience. Maybe we can use him in our newly reconfigured company."

I smiled at that thought. "I'll see what he says," I replied and dashed out the door.

I texted Rhys to make sure he was free tonight and tomorrow, and when he said he was, I hurried back to Wilcox to share my news.

"So," I said, across from him at the pizza place, "what do you think?"

Rhys smiled. "I think it's a great opportunity, but Xander, you're going to be working more, not less. You understand that, right?" he asked.

I nodded. "Yeah, I do, and you know I didn't plan this. It just fell into my lap. Besides, I have to work. My projects in Wilcox aren't going to work out, so would you… well, could you consider at some point—not now, of course, but you know, in the future—would you consider moving closer to Portland? We could even move to Salem, which would be closer to Wilcox and Portland."

Rhys studied his soda. "My life is here, Xander. I left Portland because I didn't want to live there. I wanted Wilcox. I gutted and rehabbed my aunt's house, my dad and stepmother have moved back here, and I have my sisters. I can't see myself moving."

I nodded and swallowed hard. I'd had a feeling that would be his reaction. "Yeah, I get it. I don't like it, but I get it."

Rhys continued to stare at his glass. "Xander, we have to consider whether this is going to work. I mean, I love you, of course I do, but we're going to be living different lives and nowhere near each other."

I didn't acknowledge what he said. I couldn't bear the thought of losing him. We'd just started this thing between us. Would I really lose him?

"I… don't decide yet. Let me get my feet wet and see what happens. Who knows, it might work." I rubbed my hand over his and felt sick when he didn't look up. He wasn't thinking about giving us more time. "Rhys, seriously, don't break up with me—not yet, not until we know how things are going to happen."

"Xander, you'll want more than an occasional hookup. You said you wanted exclusivity, but how can we have that when we're hours apart? Don't you think we're better off just pulling back and letting ourselves pursue our careers? If you were going to be here, it'd be different. But you aren't, are you?" I hadn't seen Rhys upset before, not like this, but I could tell he was barely holding it together. "I'm going to go home and let this settle. I'm sorry, Xander, I need to think. I'll… I'll see you tomorrow," he said, and he left before the pizza arrived.

I stared at the pie that came shortly after. *What the fuck just happened?* I wondered. Surely, after such an amazing time together, I wouldn't lose him now.

Rhys

I KEPT REMEMBERING the dream of me on the cliff far from Xander, and the gulf between us widening until there was nothing but impenetrable vastness.

I was happy he'd found his dream job, but I wasn't ready to give up my home to chase his dreams with him. Hell, we were just beginning to date. We'd only just admitted we had feelings. It seemed like providence was keeping us apart.

I pulled into the driveway and walked up to the door. When I opened it, I felt the breeze hit me. "Go back," I heard, and my heartbeat kicked up as I immediately remembered the journal. This was the fucking same thing, or at least similar to what happened to Aunt Helen and Greta, Xander's aunt.

"No, Aunt Helen," I said to her ghost. "I need to figure this out. I can't be chasing rainbows. I have family to think about."

I sat down on the sofa then and let the tears come. I must've wept for at least an hour before Dad and Lucy came in with the girls. I quickly wiped my tears so as not to alarm my sisters, but Dad and Lucy noticed.

Lucy took the girls upstairs while Dad grabbed a box of tissues and came over. "Here, you look like you could use this." He handed me the box.

I nodded. "Thanks, Dad," I croaked.

"So, wanna talk about it?" he asked.

"I guess," I said, then wiped my eyes with a tissue and blew my nose. "Xander got offered an even better job with his company. I told him I didn't know how we could be together if he wasn't going to be in town. Then, when I got here, I remembered Aunt Helen and… well, her and Greta."

If Dad thought that sounded strange, he showed no sign.

"He… he wants me to move to Portland."

Dad sighed and leaned back on the sofa. "Listen, can I offer you some advice?" he asked, and I nodded.

"I screwed up with your mom. I was so pigheaded I could only see things happening my way. By the time I realized, I'd pushed her so far she was unable to forgive me. I'm lucky because I found Lucy, and we've got an amazing relationship, but I almost did the same thing to her." He was silent for a moment, then hiccupped with emotion. "Rhys, I almost lost her. I was so focused on my career and the next project that I missed how important it is to have my family with me. Our aunt made the same mistake with Greta. Her parents did the same thing with her and my mom. We've destroyed relationships, focused on the wrong things. Tell me, why is it so important for you to remain here, in Wilcox?" he asked.

"You, Lucy, the girls, this house—"

"All will be right here when and if you ever return."

"What about the hardware store?" I asked.

"We're fine, Rhys. Don't use us as an excuse to throw away a chance at true love. Xander is a good man. You seem to be as crazy about him as he is about you. If you love him, don't throw away your happiness over perceived roadblocks."

He clapped me on the knee and went upstairs to Lucy and the girls.

I wandered down the stairs and fell into bed. I had another little cry, but this time it was over what I'd be giving up when I moved back to Portland to be with Xander. Dad made sense, and I think I knew that even before we talked. I wasn't going to throw away our future just because I was being stubborn.

That night I asked if Dad minded if Xander and I stayed in my apartment over the garage while his house was on the market.

"You can have the whole house, since we've taken over yours," he said.

That sounded perfect, so, ready with a new plan, I walked across the bridge to Xander's ugly house and knocked on the door.

When he opened it, I smiled. "Okay. I'm in."

"Huh?" He looked confused.

"If you're going to be in Portland, so am I. I'll call the company that bought Dad out and see if they can use an electrician."

His eyes bugged. "You're serious? Really?" he asked, and I smiled.

"Come kiss me, Xander. This was a hard decision," I lamented.

He rushed me then and grabbed me up into his arms. "Rhys, oh God, I love you so much. I didn't think you would."

"Yeah, me either, but a certain ghost had other ideas. We agreed not to make the same mistakes, didn't we?"

He nodded. "Okay, this is me not making the same mistake." Xander kissed me and dragged me into his house. "Then, this is me," he said, jerking his shirt off, "showing you my gratitude. Oh my God, I'm about to rock your fucking world."

I laughed as he picked me up and tossed me onto the sofa.

I had to fight not to get emotional as Xander indeed rocked my world. I was so in love with him. How had that happened in such a short time? I would never know. What I did know was that, as much as it hurt to leave Wilcox, Xander Petterson was worth the sacrifice.

Xander

THE FIRST few weeks after Rhys agreed to move in with me, the world seemed to click into place. Rhys and I moved into his father's home, which he and Lucy decided to pull off the market since they were going to stay in Rhys's place back in Wilcox.

Rhys bounced between Wilcox and Portland but decided not to take another job until he finished the barn conversion. The time back in Wilcox seemed to help the transition for him. It certainly helped me, since I had him in our shared bed over the weekends.

I missed Wilcox and Mom. I hated that, especially knowing Rhys had sacrificed home to be with me. Luckily Mom could come up and stay because we had the huge house to ourselves.

I was happy we'd made it happen before the official merger of Hendrix and Direct. I figured the work would be much worse, but I was wrong. In fact, as Direct's management began to come in to Hendrix, they did the opposite of giving over projects. They immediately began to take over our projects, but not with a positive effect.

I complained to James a week into the merger, and he shook his head. "Just give it time, Xander. Stand your ground. We knew there'd be growing pains."

By the time we were a month in, balls were being dropped by their overeager and aggressive management. I ended up firing two men from Direct who were supposed to be under me, only to have one of the Direct owners hire them back and tell me I didn't have the right to fire people who came from their company.

"Then I can't manage them," I said. I would've quit then and there had James not talked me off the cliff. That and I remembered I'd already uprooted Rhys. I couldn't just throw my job out the window when he'd given up so much.

The fall sucked. Even my ever-efficient assistant was showing signs of wear. I kept my mouth shut like when I'd worked with Leon, letting balls get dropped and projects fall through the cracks. I took the brunt of the blame, even though everyone—James, Mr. Hendrix, and the other two owners—knew it was their decision to keep the incompetent managers at fault.

The holidays came and went, and life continued to get worse and almost unbearable. When spring was closing in, and our work at the company was finally beginning to slow, I found out what was really going on with the merger. Just before Easter, James pulled me into his office and told me he and his father were stepping down. "We will be private stockholders but no longer manage the company ourselves."

I sighed. "James, I feel like I've been set up. Did you know this was happening from the beginning?" I could tell by the look on his face that he did. "I can't promise I'm going to stay. Not after the fiasco this has been, but we'll see."

"Xander?" he said, and I turned back toward him. "I'm sorry, I honestly didn't know the Direct guys would be this difficult."

I sighed. "None of us did, James."

I waved him off and called my mother as soon as I was in my office. "Hey, what's up?" she asked.

"Shit, lots of shit. Hey, can you have your cleaning crew spruce up my house? I want to spend a few days down in Wilcox, and I have a feeling Rhys will too."

"Sure, anything in particular making it shit?" she asked, coming back to the subject.

I laughed. "Sort of. I dragged Rhys all the way back to Portland. Now I'm thinking about quitting," I said, speaking quietly enough that I didn't alert any of the employees around me of my thoughts.

"Wow, that bad, huh?"

"Mom, it's worse than bad. I have no authority. The upper management is undermining me. I should've known it was too good to be true."

Mom chuckled. "If it looks too good to be true, it usually is. Okay, son, I'll call to see if they can do it. When do you want to come back?"

"Not sure. Let me talk to Rhys and find out," I said, and after she shared her typical Wilcox gossip, she told me how much she was enjoying her new position as county commissioner. There had been so much mismanagement by the previous administration that she'd worked almost full-time since she took over. Good thing her real estate job didn't require much of her time this early in the year or she'd have been overwhelmed cleaning up the mess she stepped into.

Now that she was in that position, it was becoming clear the former commissioner was in so far over his head that when Levi and I painted those bridges, he had seen it as someone calling him out. It made sense why he hated us—me—so much now.

Oh well, if anyone could put the county to rights, it was my mother. The woman was nothing if not organized.

I let my project managers know I'd be taking time away from the office. "Call if you need me," I said, knowing the two troublemakers would take it as their chance to force themselves further into my business. Oh well, it couldn't be helped. I needed to figure out what I was going to do, and I needed to spend time with Rhys to know what he thought about it.

It seemed inconceivable, but I'd been officially living with Rhys for almost five months. Still, we hadn't seen each other enough for me to know how he would feel if I left my job. Mostly we fucked and slept when I had time off.

Not that he ever complained. Rhys wasn't a complainer. He was a doer, a fixer. I couldn't help but think I'd made the biggest mistake a man could make—I'd taken a job that didn't respect me or the work I put in, and I'd managed to pull my sweet lover into my drama. God, I hoped I could fix that, and soon.

Rhys

"THINGS GETTING any better?" Dad asked as he walked through the almost completed barn conversion. He was helping me tape out the problem areas that still needed to be fixed—the famous last step in any construction project.

"No, I still barely see him. I'm glad we have time together, but he's like a zombie when he's off, and they call him when they don't need to and don't when they do."

Dad laughed. "That sounds familiar. All part of running a large company."

"That's what you were trying to get me to do before I moved here," I said, sort of off the cuff.

Dad stopped and looked at me. "No, well, maybe. You're good at managing these projects. Just look at this. It's amazing."

I smiled. It was amazing. I loved working with Cliff and Brandon. They'd given me all the space I needed when the project started. Then they quickly made decisions. They were also more than a little gifted with design. The place was outstanding and beautiful.

I knew they were going to make it an amazing home. I had to bite down on my jealousy since I knew that as long as Xander worked his ridiculous hours, we wouldn't be making a home like this ourselves.

I was pleased when Dad and I were done. There weren't many things to fix, and the crew already knew most of them.

I followed Dad out of the house, called my guys, and told them what we'd found. "Got it, boss," my head guy said. "We'll knock those out tomorrow. Then that's it, right?"

I looked at the landscaping and wished Brandon had let me hire a crew to fix it, but both he and Cliff were determined to do the yard work themselves. "Yep. We're done after this. I want to give the keys to Brandon and Cliff by the weekend."

"Yep, got it. We'll make it happen."

I chuckled. "They're great guys. Too bad Xander's project didn't work out. I hate the thought of losing this crew to another company."

Dad winked at me. "One never knows what the future holds, but you're right, these guys are better than average." He clapped me on the back as we looked up at the new building. "Job very well done, son."

When we got back to Wilcox, I saw activity over at Xander's place and crossed the bridge to check it out. I knew he wanted to tear the house down, but no one wanted vagrants living in their home. I was pulling my phone out in case I needed to call 911 when I noticed Dan, the guy who cleaned houses for Xander's mom.

"Hey, Dan, what's up?" I asked.

"Oh, Xander asked our crew to come clean. Are you boys finally gonna sell this monstrosity?" he asked.

I shook my head. "Not sure, Dan. I haven't heard if that's what he's wanting to do."

"Well, never mind. We'll clean it up as best we can," he said, and I watched as he and his crew went inside.

Was Xander considering selling? That thought depressed me more than I could swallow. If I'd moved up to Portland to be with him, even part-time, didn't that mean he should at least tell me when he wanted to sell?

I shook it off. No need to get bent out of shape until I talked to him. Even if it did bite. I texted him.

Just saw Dan over at your house. Said he was cleaning. Thought you'd like to know.

I went on in and thought maybe I'd get a text back. When I didn't, I felt myself getting angry. Irrational? Maybe, maybe not. Regardless, I needed to talk with my boyfriend before things got ugly inside me.

I didn't hear from Xander until after seven. When he called, he told me he had to resolve a crisis at work before he could come home. "Come home? To Wilcox?" I asked.

"Oh shit, sorry Rhys, I meant to touch base with you this afternoon, then the shit hit the fan. Yeah, I took time off. I need to discuss a few things with you, and I can't do that when we're apart." I had to bite my tongue not to say something about us being in different places because he took a job that keeps him busy twenty-four-seven. Yeah, I was still upset about him selling his house. If he was. Maybe he wasn't. I was upset about being stuck in Portland. I think seeing the cleaning crew was just the catalyst that forced me to admit it.

"Okay, see you when you get here," I said. Then I hung up so I didn't accidentally blow up until I had all the details. Besides, he was coming to Wilcox. Maybe that's why they were cleaning. So why wasn't I cooling off?

That was evidence I was mad about something else. *Best walk it off*, I thought. I told Dad I was going for a walk, jumped in the truck, and drove over to the park where Xander and I had hiked during the summer.

I had already begun to think of it as our spot. Maybe if I could get through the mud and up to the view, I could figure out what was going on. The winter had been wet, which was great, considering all the wildfires in the past few years.

Hell, poor Cliff had lost his home in California due to the fires. I forced myself not to mumble about the wet ground as I thought of that.

I didn't make it to the top of the mountain. I slipped and fell, almost busted my knee on a boulder, and decided I needed to cool the fuck off. Besides, it would be too dark to see by the time I made it to the top. There were bears and mountain lions here too. I needed to walk back.

I had just turned around when a bluebird landed on a branch no more than six feet in front of me.

I froze. Oregon's bluebirds were gorgeous. You never saw them in town, and in the country, they were skittish. My hand itched to pull my phone out and photograph it. I knew if I did, I'd chase it off.

Instead I stood rooted to the muddy spot as the pretty little bird ruffled its feathers, sang a sweet little tune, then flitted off into the distance. Tears dripped on my hand before I even realized I was crying. I wasn't angry at Xander, not really. I was angry about our situation. I didn't want to live in Portland. I loved Wilcox with its natural beauty.

That little bluebird was a reminder of that. I had spent the past five months driving back and forth from Portland with little to show for it except a considerable gasoline bill, a truck that was rapidly adding up the miles, and a boyfriend who only had snippets of time to spend with me.

"Things have to change," I said out loud and wiped at the tears. I hadn't cried in years. Now I'd found myself weeping twice in the last six months. Not that they hadn't been a good six months. I did have Xander when he was free, and I loved him. I loved him so much. Lucy was better, and the doctors thought she was in remission again. They just had to do a few more tests to make sure.

The girls loved school here and told Dad they didn't want to move back to Portland. I found myself enjoying the barn conversion more than I ever thought possible. I'd resisted managing projects all the time I worked with Dad, but now I knew that was the very thing I wanted to do.

I had to fess up to Xander, and his having a few days off was the perfect opportunity.

I mostly felt my way back down the wet, soggy path to my car, and I laughed at my mud-caked legs and boots. *What was I thinking?*

"Thinking you needed to get some *thinking* done," I said to myself. By the time I drove home and pulled into the driveway, the lights were out in the living room, so I assumed everyone was in bed or at least in their bedrooms. I went around back, not worrying about getting muddy now that I was covered, and slipped through my back door, unloaded my stuff in the laundry room, and stripped to keep from tracking in mud.

When I came out, I was stark naked and almost had a freaking heart attack. "Hey," Xander said from my couch.

"For the fucking love of God, why didn't you say something? Jeez, you just about scared the life out of me," I said.

Xander came over and put his arms on my shoulders. "You look good," he said, and he scanned up and down my naked body.

"Is that so?" I asked.

"Yep, and I didn't say anything, afraid I would scare you. You look frozen, though. Let's get you into the shower."

I didn't argue as Xander pulled me into the bathroom, turned the hot water on, and stripped himself.

He felt so good as he slipped behind me and held me as we stood under the hot water. When my waterworks started again, Xander turned me around and faced me. "Honey, what's wrong? Why're you crying?"

I shook my head to get myself under control. "Let's just go get into the hot tub. I need to talk to you."

Xander looked alarmed, and I could understand why. I didn't even have the energy to tell him I wasn't breaking up with him. It seemed serious enough that it could have that effect if it didn't go well.

He nodded, and knowing my family wasn't likely to come down, we climbed into the hot tub without finding shorts. "Okay, what's going on?" Xander asked as he knelt in front of me.

I took a deep breath and steeled myself. "Xander, I can't keep doing the Portland thing. I'm so sorry. I tried, but today I thought you'd decided to sell the house when I found Dan over there cleaning. It's like, to me, that was the last straw. The last hope that you'd be coming back to Wilcox. I don't want to keep coming up there and you not have time for me when all I want to do is crawl into this tub, snuggle with you, and enjoy a simple life. I know you're ambitious. I love that about you, but—"

"Shhh," he said, putting his finger over my lips. "You just answered the question I came home to ask," he said. "Rhys, honey, I felt so guilty. I want to quit my job. I hate it. It's the worst job ever, and my former bosses are retiring or taking a back seat, whatever. I felt like I uprooted your life, dragged you out of your home, and now I was going to quit. It felt like I was disrespecting you and your sacrifice."

I just stared at him. "You're kidding me. How long have you wanted to quit?" I asked.

He looked down and shrugged. "Three months or so, if I'm honest. I knew when the Direct guy undermined my authority, it wouldn't work out. Rhys, please don't be angry. I mean, I was—"

I didn't let him get the words out. Instead I launched myself into his arms. "So you're quitting, like, for real? You're going to tell them to shove it?" I asked, causing him to laugh.

"Oh yeah, I can't wait to tell them to shove it."

"Woo hoo!" I yelled, not caring if I woke the twins. "That's the best news I've had all year, but… but are you wanting to come here, to live in Wilcox?" I asked, needing him to confirm that he and I were on the same page.

He nodded. "I have to work. I don't know where that'll be yet, but Roseburg isn't far, and neither is Eugene. Even if I have to drive there, it'll be better than Portland and working for Direct Construction. I want to be here, yes. This is our home, Rhys."

The waterworks sprang again, this time because I was so fucking relieved. We got out and, still wet, pulled each other into the house. Xander fucked me as I sang his name. His strong hands embraced me, making me feel loved and complete. When we both came at the same time, we fell over and spooned.

"I love you, Xander. I didn't know what we were going to do, but I knew I loved you. My God, I'm so fucking relieved."

Xander chuckled behind me. "I love you too, Rhys," he said, and we lay there slipping in and out of sleep until I stood and pulled him into bed. God help me, if I had anything to say about it, this would be our bed and bedroom from now on.

Xander

IT'D BEEN a month since Rhys handed the keys to Brandon and Cliff. They were both so ecstatic they glowed. I could understand why. They'd been living in that tiny trailer for so long, and now they had this absolutely gorgeous barn conversion my sweet Rhys had built for them.

I told James via phone that I was quitting and that I'd send him a letter of resignation. He told me it wasn't necessary. The Direct guys had been spying on me and heard me tell Mom I was considering quitting.

The idiots had put one of the troublemakers into my position before I even officially resigned. Not that I cared. Karma was headed their way like a bullet from hell.

Oren, bless his heart, collected my things and sent them to me. I swear I needed to buy the guy flowers or something. He'd made my life a shit-ton easier.

The open house was packed. The Owens family was here, of course, as was Brandon's faux uncle, who was insane but funnier than shit. They had leveled the yard, and grass was beginning to grow. Brandon had also created several beautiful flower gardens.

Brandon was such a contradiction from our childhood. He'd become a college professor, turned novelist, and now was a best-selling author. Cliff was clearly the love of his life, but Cliff worked like a dog while Brandon became a domesticated spouse.

It was strange but sweet. "Whattaya think?" I heard the devil himself ask.

I smiled. "I think it's more amazing than I ever dreamed."

"It is. We love it. Your guy has a gift," Brandon said.

I winked at him. "He really does, Brandon?" I said when I saw Cliff come up behind him. "I want you to know, this makes me happy. Mom too. She can speak for herself, but after my aunt passed away, this was a sad reminder of her difficult life. You've turned it into something amazing. Thanks for that."

Brandon looked at Cliff, and the two smiled at me. "Thanks, Xander. I don't think it would've happened, and certainly not as fast as it has, if it weren't for your suggestion and encouragement to get Rhys to take us on."

I nodded. That was for sure.

I watched Mom and attorney Tim's wife, Polly, our new mayor, walk toward us. "Hey, guys, this house is amazing. I never would've thought an old barn could turn into this," Mom said.

Brandon and Cliff smiled and hugged the two women. They were chatting when I began to look around for Rhys. I was just about to excuse myself when Ms. Polly slipped her arm through mine. "May I borrow you for a moment?" she asked.

"For you, Ms. Polly, anytime," I said, and she led me to where Rhys was talking to his father.

"Hey, gentlemen, I wonder if you'd mind showing me the outside," Polly said as she opened the door and breezed through without waiting for an answer.

I glanced at Mark and Rhys, and when they shrugged, we all followed her out.

"Isn't this the most lovely spot? I remember when Greta lived here by herself. I used to come out with Ms. Helen when I was a kid. Back then, they did Girl Scout stuff together, and we'd come here to do badge work. I never would've dreamed this could look so good," Polly said.

None of us responded as we waited for her to tell us why we were out here. She turned to us and winked. "I'm going to get straight to the point. I want you to resubmit your request to build next to the covered bridge. Your mother, Xander, told me you're also interested in developing the land across from Rhys's place. That's good, 'cause the state just informed us the river needs to be shored up behind the house you bought before it creates problems for our sewerage systems."

"Wait, so you want me to develop that side of the river too?"

"Of course. Your mother said that was your original plan. Now listen, I know my predecessor and his minions gave you a hard time. That was because of the county commissioner. The city was getting grant money that had to come through the county, and the son of a bitch had blackmailed them into keeping the money away if they didn't... well, do what they did to you. It was unacceptable and ultimately cost most of them their positions during the last election. People were upset you didn't get to do your project. Now, seeing this today, what you did, Rhys, is going to make the townsfolk that much more upset. We need you boys to step up. You too, Mark. Folks are lumping you in with these two, and that's not a bad thing. So, what say you? Are you willing to take on another project?"

I just laughed. "Sometimes I think the universe is just screwing with me. Ms. Polly, I just quit my job. I was going to have to find an investment outside town because I have to work, you know."

Polly clapped her hands and laughed. "Oh, this is a good day. A very good day. Oh, you need to talk to your mama too. The money from the levy is coming in, and we need to get those bridges painted and repair anything that needs to be fixed. Things are looking up for our county and Wilcox, boys, really looking up."

With a backward wave, she left us standing where we were. "Could you have imagined that?" I asked, and Mark smiled. "I had a feeling it was just a matter of time. Congrats, Xander." He clapped me on the shoulder and walked back inside.

"We can get that resubmitted by Monday. Xander, if there's any way, I really would like to work with you to build new homes in Wilcox."

"Oh yeah, there's a way. I have to see if my funding partners are still willing, but even if they aren't, the revenues for a project like this are well worth the financial risk. I think we can find someone to take it on."

"And the property across from me? We need to get all that drawn up. I have no idea what the city has to do to shore up the riverbank, but strike when the iron is hot, right?"

I reached down and patted his cute little ass. "Oh, I know all about striking when your iron is hot."

Rhys

"I'M SO happy for you—for us—Xander," I said the day the approval showed up in his email. He grabbed me and swung me around like I didn't weigh anything, and I laughed like I always did.

"It's really going to happen. After all these years and all this preparation, it's finally happening," Xander said.

"It is, and you deserve it."

"We deserve it," he corrected as he leaned down for a kiss. "You did amazing work over at Brandon and Cliff's. The town noticed. They know you're going to help me build this, and of course, like Ms. Polly said, your dad is too. They know we're going to do amazing work, and it's going to be our project. Yours and mine."

Xander kissed me and then twirled me again. We were just about to take things to another level when the doorbell rang.

"Ignore it," Xander whispered.

"No, it could be important," I said and dashed upstairs.

Xander's mom came in, smiling from ear to ear. "Has he gotten the email?" she asked.

I laughed. "Yep, we were just celebrating," I said. Then I blushed when I realized I was telling his mom we were about to bone each other.

She chuckled. "Okay, forgive me, but there's a lot of people wanting to celebrate. I put most of them off, but not all."

She looked behind her and waved. Polly and Tim—our mayor and the attorney—stood off to the side. Jason Murrin, who worked for Tim, was there too, as were Brandon, Cliff, Levi, and Keya, Levi's wife.

"What are y'all doing? We can't party in the middle of the morning."

"Says who?" Polly slapped my hand playfully. "Can we come in? We have coffee and danish. Oh, your father's coming too. Stewie said he can hold the fort while your stepmom and your dad come celebrate."

I couldn't help but laugh. This was our town. "I'll go get Xander," I said, hoping to God he didn't come up the stairs in his birthday suit. I didn't think he would, mostly because we shared the house with my family, but still.

"Um, honey," I said when I got downstairs.

I about popped a blood vessel when I saw he was lying stark naked on my bed waiting for me.

"Um, you might have to put that thought on the back burner. We have guests. A lot of guests."

"What? Who? No, don't tell me, Mom and Polly?"

"That's Mayor Polly now, and not just them. Get dressed and come up. They want to celebrate with you."

Xander sighed, but he smiled. That was the nature of Wilcox, and we both knew it.

We came back up to find Xander's mom and Polly had taken over the house. There were treats on the kitchen counter, coffee cups had been pulled down, and my dad and Lucy stood in the corner smiling like kids at their birthday party.

"Rhys, Xander," Lucy said when she saw us. She pulled us into a hug. "I'm so happy for you two."

"Well, it should be a celebration for more than us. Hey, all, Lucy got some good news yesterday that's worth celebrating too." Everyone turned around, and Lucy blushed. "Sorry for putting you on the spot, but this is important, and, well, this is our community," I said.

She nodded. "I'm officially cancer-free—no sign of it anywhere. They've run extra tests. It's just nowhere to be seen."

"What? Oh, Lucy," Xander's mom came over to embrace her. Of course, Polly followed shortly behind, and then the guys. "This really is a celebration," she said.

"Okay, so you got approval. What does that mean? When can you start?" Jason asked. "I'm so excited. I've never been involved in a project like this before. Of course, Tim's handling most of the background stuff, but… well, I'm excited," he said.

Xander smiled. "We have to get all the plans back in place, get the crews set up, tear down that monstrosity of a house, then go from there."

"Not to mention," Polly said, coming up behind us, "we have to figure out that mess with the river. I'm pretty sure we can get grants through the state for that, but of course that'll have to go through our new commissioner," Polly said, smiling at Xander's mom.

"One thing at a time. First, the project on that side of the river. Then we'll focus on this side. Right, son?" she asked.

"Yes, boss," he said, and she slapped him on the bicep.

The morning was fun. Jason, Brandon, and Cliff didn't know each other well. Jason was younger than I was, so they hadn't known each other before everyone disappeared off to their careers. But he was a cool guy. I knew Tim would probably be retiring soon, or at least the gossip from the hardware store seemed to think so.

Jason would be taking over, or at least I assumed he would. It paid to know your local attorney. And the way Jason and Cliff were teasing one another, I guessed a friendship was budding.

By the time Dad and Lucy had to return to the store, the rest of the group had begun to disperse. I locked the front door and drew Xander down to the basement so I could start where we'd been forced to leave off. Today was a day to celebrate, and I couldn't think of any better way than making love with my boyfriend.

Xander

"GOD, MOM, I'm so nervous. What if he says no?"

"You're insane. That boy isn't going to say no. Besides, you're the dingbat who had to make it a big community spectacle. You could still do it later, just you and him."

"Ugh," I moaned. "No, this feels right. Rhys is firmly ensconced in Wilcox, and I am now too. If I'm going to ask him to marry me, I should do it in front of his family and friends. I'm not even sure why that's so important. I just know it is."

Mom kissed my cheek. "Son, you do what you feel is right. Now, do you have the ring?" she asked.

I patted my dress pants pocket, almost freaking out until I found it. "Yeah, it's here. Got it."

"Okay, let's go."

She tugged me out of the house just as Rhys, Mark, and Lucy came across the bridge. Mayor Polly, Tim, Jason, Brandon, Cliff, Levi, Keya, the Owenses, and several council members were also there. I saw a few neighbors come out of their houses and make their way toward the festivities.

It was five minutes before go time, and we were already building a fairly big crowd—much bigger than I anticipated. People in Wilcox took an interest in things they considered important.

I was sweating bullets, not because of the ribbon cutting, but because I was second-guessing my decision to ask Rhys to marry me in front of that many people. Rhys came up and slipped his arm around me, and suddenly the world tilted back on its axis. Yeah, fuck me. It was very right.

"Ladies and gentlemen," Polly said, catching everyone's attention, "today is a very special occasion. As we all know, the house behind us represented the end of an era in our community. Most of us have despaired of the home since it was built. Now the area is at the beginning of a new era. One that will change this part of Wilcox for the better. Xander, can you come up here and say a few words?"

I nodded and walked up to the mic. "Hi, all, and thanks for coming out today. This has been a dream of mine for a very long time. It's been a while since Wilcox had a housing project in the downtown area. Well, it's been a long time since any large-scale housing was built in Wilcox," I said, getting a few snickers from the crowd. "That's about to change. We desperately need new housing. We don't want to be like other towns, though, where modern homes detract from the local character. Rhys and I will bring you homes with porches for neighbors to sit on—places where kids can enjoy time away from their PlayStations. Wilcox is now and has always been about community. That's what this development will support."

The crowd clapped enthusiastically, which was pretty good for this type of gathering.

"As you know, Rhys renovated his late aunt's home, just across the river from this development. I grew up not far from here, and we both have a vested interest in our town. So, before we go, I would like to take a moment to do something that, well, that—"

I got emotional, and Mom put her hand on my arm. "Rhys," I said and turned to him. "I love you, not just because you're the most handsome man in the world, but because you're smart and witty. You're a hard worker who believes in your town and your heritage. I learn from you every day and thank the universe for allowing me to be a part of your life."

Rhys smiled but looked a bit suspicious. God, please don't let this be a bad idea, I pleaded.

"I almost made the mistake of taking you away from Wilcox. A mistake that would've been a detriment to both of us, to our families, and, ultimately, to everyone standing here with us today. You came with me, sacrificing everything for us. I will never forget that. Today we start a new chapter, not just in Wilcox but for you and me. Forgive me if I'm overstepping," I said, dropping to my knee, "but would you please consider being my husband?"

Rhys' eyes grew big, and his mouth formed a perfect O while what was happening registered in his head. "Are you proposing to me in front of your ribbon cutting?" he asked.

"Oh yeah, I'm totally doing that."

Rhys leaned back and laughed out loud. "My God, Xander, of course I'll marry you."

I jumped up and kissed him right in front of the town. I heard Polly say something to the crowd, but I no longer cared. Rhys had just agreed to be my husband, to marry me and make our lives complete, and that was the best news I'd ever had.

I pulled back and showed Rhys the rings I'd bought. My dad's family was Scottish and very proud of the fact. While in Millersville, I'd discovered a craftsman, a distant cousin. He specialized in Scottish jewelry and agreed to make me two thistle rings for my engagement. He even said he could make them so they locked into a wedding ring later.

Of course it was perfect, and when I showed them to Rhys, his face lit up. "Dang, Xander, these are amazing."

I slipped one on his finger and the matching one on mine. Mom, Rhys's family, and Polly were the only ones who stayed behind. "Did I chase everyone off?" I asked.

Polly laughed. "No, I sent them to the café for pie. I'm afraid you'll have to go over now or they and the rest of the town will be here to see those rings. I'm sure the grapevine has informed everyone of your engagement."

"We might need a moment, but we'll be there," Rhys said, causing Polly to wink at us.

"No time for a full romp, for real. If you don't show up after cutting the ribbon and proposing, they'll all show up at your house anyway."

Rhys laughed. "They will. She's not wrong."

I kissed him again. "Okay, we'll make an appearance. Then I'm whisking my fiancé off to do naughty things to him."

Polly laughed. "Congratulations, boys, on both life-changing events." She kissed us both on the cheek, then Tim shook our hands, she led him to their car, and they took off toward the café.

Mom came over and hugged us. "Welcome to the family, Rhys. I'm such a lucky woman. Now I'm going to have two sons to love." She wiped a tear and kissed us. Then she headed to the café herself.

Dad and Lucy both hugged us as well. "Your mom's going to be so pissed," Lucy said. "Lucky for you, I recorded the whole thing and already texted her."

"Um, in my defense, I didn't know he was going to propose," Rhys said, which got a chuckle from Mark.

"You better call her first thing. Lucy isn't wrong. She's going to be unhappy she missed this."

I cringed. "Sorry, I should've invited her, but I was a nervous wreck. Ask my mom. I've been sweating bullets."

"You didn't do anything wrong. That was a beautiful proposal," Lucy said. "It'll be the talk of the town from now on," she added. Lucy might not be from here, but she fit Wilcox life like a glove.

Mark and Lucy left, and I pulled Rhys back into the house. "Are you mad?" I asked the moment the door shut.

"Oh, no way. You are the sweetest man I know, fiancé," he said.

"You sure we can't blow the town folk off? I want to get you naked right now."

Rhys kissed me. "Should've thought of that before asking me in front of the town, but we don't have to stay long, and when we get home, we're going to have to stay here and not at my house because when I get you alone, you're not going to be able to stay quiet."

The saliva abandoned my mouth and my cock grew just thinking of what he was going to do to me that made me too loud to be in his house. "Good," I whispered, "'cause I plan to tear this thing down sooner rather than later. We should send her off with a flourish, don't you think?"

Epilogue

Rhys

"MOM, PLEASE, I get it. You're upset you missed the proposal, but for real, I don't think he was thinking about which family I'd have here."

"He could've asked," she complained.

"Why don't you come down this weekend and we'll have a family celebration. You can even be in charge."

"Oh, Rhys, yes. I like that idea. We'll bring all the accoutrements," she said, and I smiled at how easy it was to distract Mom with a party. As much as I didn't love them, she did.

I immediately called Dad and let him know Mom was going to blow in with an engagement party, not that she wouldn't have already called Lucy the moment she hung up with me. I swear those two got closer every day.

I called Xander next. "Hi, honey, whatcha doing?" I asked when he answered.

"Hi back at you. I'm talking to the demolition company. Who knew it was this much work to tear down a house?"

"Well, I did, but that's because I've done a few. So, Mom's coming in and throwing us a party, and um, she's miffed about missing the engagement, so we might have to make it a big deal."

Xander chuckled. "I'm sorry I didn't invite her. I just got carried away. Yeah, a party sounds fun. When?"

"Um, not sure. I'll text her later, when she's had some time to work through the details." I heard someone talking to Xander, and he had to let me go. Getting the house ready to demo should be my thing if I was going to be his project manager, but now that he wasn't working in Portland, I figured he'd be taking on more of the project. I didn't mind, as long as it meant he'd be here with me.

I didn't have much on my plate today, so I spent time with Dad and Lucy at the hardware store. Our new merchandise had come in and was already selling like hotcakes.

No one could argue that Lucy didn't have an eye for retail. Stewie was still out on his honeymoon leave, and I didn't expect to see him around much now. He was certainly enjoying his new married life. But he had every right to retire, after keeping this place running for so many years.

That meant Dad had to spend his time at the register. I immediately took on inventory almost every time I came into work, and of course we were in danger of selling out of a lot of stuff.

Once done, I went to the front to give Dad a break. I sat on the stool and surveyed the store. I could see all the changes that had been implemented since I had arrived.

I checked out one of our regulars and was about to begin organizing the snacks when Mayor Polly, a name I was trying to force myself to say now, came up to the register.

"I just want you boys to know how much we appreciate all you've done here in Wilcox. The hardware store looks fabulous, and you've added everything," she said, and I smiled.

"Thanks, Mayor. So, is there any gossip from city hall?"

"Oh, not from me. I have to be responsible these days. I'm afraid you'll have to get your gossip from other sources now." I laughed, knowing that would never be a problem in Wilcox. "Really though, Rhys, Helen would've been so proud of you and your father. You've shone a bright light on a fading place. We need a lot more of that in Wilcox—a whole lot more."

"You need to sit down with Xander and hear some of his ideas. I won't repeat anything he's told me, but Wilcox is going to grow. We're in too valuable a spot this close to Interstate 5. The issue, of course, is how we control and manipulate that growth so it doesn't destroy our spirit."

"Well said, young man. You might have a future in politics if you keep talking like that."

I laughed. "Nope, not my cup of tea. But I love my hometown, and I'd like to see it grow sensibly. No major box stores destroying what few small businesses we've managed to keep."

Mayor Polly winked at me and took her purchases to leave. We really had made a difference here in Wilcox. I think Aunt Helen must've known we could. I had no idea how the future would play out, but I looked forward to it even more, knowing I'd be walking into it with my beloved fiancé, Xander Petterson.

Xander

RHYS'S HOUSE was decked out for the party. The fact that people flowed in and out of the house in an organized way made me think Rhys's mom missed her calling as a party organizer.

Most of the guests had left, and just our small crowd, including my mother, the attorney, our new mayor, and Rhys's family, were seated around the living room. "Xander, please, if you've got your blueprints for the new houses, can you show them to me?" Rhys's mom said.

"Um, sure," I replied and rushed down to Rhys's lower level, where I'd moved in, and grabbed the preliminary blueprints. I handed them to Linda, who spread them on the big coffee table in the middle of the room.

Mark cocked an eyebrow, and I got a clue this was unusual. "Oh, look at this one, Johney. I love the wide front porch. How many square feet is it?" she asked. I would've responded, but Johney was already looking through the prints. "Sixteen hundred with an unfinished attic?" he asked, looking up at me.

I nodded, as I was almost sure that was correct.

"Can you give us a sweet lower basement level like Rhys has here?"

"Um, sure. You?" I asked.

"Yes," Linda said, sitting back. "I'm not going to miss another major event in my son's life. If you all are moving here to stay, by God, so are we." She crossed her arms defensively.

"Mom, that's quite a move. I thought you hated small towns."

"Oh, Rhys, I did when you were younger. It felt claustrophobic. But now I work mostly from home. Besides," she looked over toward my mother, who smiled and nodded, "Ellen has offered me a job as her assistant. She's busy with her new position as county commissioner, and I've had my Oregon real estate license for over twenty years. I'd love to help you boys sell these homes—at least the ones we're not buying ourselves." She winked at Johney.

Johney looked at me apologetically and asked, "So, I know you were working with old Joe, but if we agree to purchase your first home in the development, do you mind if I make a few modifications to the blueprints? I already know a couple of ways to make the house more livable. It'll save us a headache later when Rhys's mom decides she wants it that way."

I laughed. "I mean, having you as the first to buy is pretty great."

Rhys was beaming beside me, and I could feel the emotions coming off him. He bounced off the sofa and pulled his mom into his arms. "I can't believe it. For real? You're going to move here?"

Linda sniffed. "Oh, honey, I miss you so much. Yes, of course, I want to live close, and I adore my... my, well I'm not sure what you'd call the girls to me. My god-granddaughters?" She chuckled. "I'd love to help spoil, um, I mean help raise them," she said as she winked at Lucy. Luckily the whole god-granddaughters thing had been discussed when the girls were babies, and Lucy and Mom were becoming best friends.

"So, um, I guess I should chime in here," Dad said, looking at Lucy. "You own the land across from here, the one with the tiny house?" he asked me, and I nodded.

"Lucy and I would like to purchase that spot from you. I know you want to develop the rest of the property, but we only need a half acre, the part that butts up to the bridge. We want to build there."

My mouth dropped open. I glanced over at Rhys, who stood immobile. "Um, Dad? What about your house in Portland?"

"Sold," Lucy said and giggled. "We didn't even get it back on the market when our neighbor saw you and Xander had moved out. Their cousin wanted to buy. It closed last week."

"Oh wow. So this is for real, then?"

Both Dad and Lucy nodded. I mean, it wasn't a surprise, considering they owned the hardware store. Rhys and I had guessed they'd eventually hire someone to manage it, but we were wrong, apparently.

"Um, except for the land around the bridge," I said, glancing at Mayor Polly. "That's going to be an official entrance to the bridge. We're going to create a little pocket park, not too big, nothing with swings or such, but a couple of nice benches and a place for people to picnic."

Rhys looked at me, and I could see another bout of emotions. He'd told me he and his aunt used to set up a picnic there, and she'd tell him about his family history. It just seemed appropriate.

"I'll donate some land for that on my side. But I want to put up a gazebo or something in honor of Aunt Helen," he said.

We made eye contact, and I could see how happy it made him. "Then that's a yes?" Mark asked.

"That's a hell yes. Wow, Rhys, you'll have to be on your best behavior with your dad and mom living right across from you."

"Hey, be careful, or I'll buy the land on the other side of the house," Mom said, causing the room to laugh.

"I couldn't think of anything better," Rhys said, and clearly he meant it. "When I moved here, I thought I was leaving my family behind, even though Aunt Helen's place always felt like home. Now you're all moving here and, well, nothing could make me happier." Before I knew it, the entire room had created a big pile of hugs. Just then the twins bumbled down the stairs and barreled into the mix.

I couldn't help but laugh. We had somehow become a big gangly family. Like Rhys, I wouldn't have it any other way.

The joy of our new life was dimmed only when Oren called and tried to get me to come back. It didn't take long for the karma I knew was coming to show up at their front door.

"Sorry, Oren, I'm committed here," I said. Then I hesitated. "Um, Oren, how much do you like working for Direct?"

He paused and didn't respond. I snorted despite myself. "Okay, then I'll just say this. If you were to be in search of another job… I know for a fact, a company in Wilcox would match your salary."

"Damn, I was hoping you'd say that." Oren laughed out loud. "When do you want me to start?"

We both laughed as I explained how I wanted someone to manage not only the houses we were building now but also the commercial properties I hoped to build in the future.

Life had a funny way of fixing itself. Not only would he be the best man to make all our construction and investment dreams come true, but he and I would have more than a little joy sticking it to the hateful Direct Construction guys.

Rhys

"MOM, FOR God's sake, it's a tux, not a dress. I'm not going to wear a lace shirt."

"Oh, but honey, for contrast, it'd be so beautiful."

"Mother—" I kissed her cheek. "—one day the twins will be grown and want to wear one of those fancy dresses I know you'd love to put me in. Lucy has already told me I can promise you a spot at the table when they choose the dresses. Now please, let's pick out something like flowers for you to put the lace into."

That was the last big conversation I had with her before Xander and I agreed to turn the planning over to Mom, Lucy, and Ellen. Of course Mayor Polly got involved as well.

The house Xander was tearing down was nothing less than a beast. The damned thing fought the entire way down. Luckily, it didn't have anything hazardous in it, so eventually, the company we hired just brought in a demolition ball and beat the monstrosity down.

Mom's house was under construction, and luckily Johney's drawing didn't include anything over the top. Mom mostly wanted a hot tub and a basement room like I had. In fact, the building looked a whole lot like this house on the inside. The layout was especially similar. I guess I had my mother's tastes. Thank goodness I wasn't as into expensive things as she was.

Dad had approval for his home but agreed not to poach any of our contractors until Mom's house was done. I think he was excited to have her and Johney close by. It takes a village to raise kids, and Mom loved the girls just like they were her grandchildren. Again I was surprised at how well my parents and stepparents had figured out how to get along.

The entire three acres around my house were filled with decorations for the wedding. Luckily Oregon summers were dry or I'd be afraid a storm would destroy all our moms' hard work. It truly was beautiful. Somehow, the four women had captured Xander and me to a tee.

We were both in T-shirts when the first wedding guests began to arrive. No one knew exactly how big the event was going to be, as we'd just had an open invitation. The local church had agreed to allow us to use any extra chairs we might need, so we appointed a couple of guys to be on chair duty in case we needed them.

"We should probably get ready," Xander whispered; then he nibbled on my earlobe.

"You aren't playing fair at all," I complained.

Xander chuckled. "Just giving you a taste of what's to come… husband."

I leaned back into him and basked in his warmth and love as his big, strong arms enfolded me.

"Guys, there's time for that *after* the wedding. Now go get ready," Mom said.

Xander kissed my neck, went over to the bed, and began to put his tux on, as I did the same. Mom came down a few moments later, and as promised, she and Ellen attached our boutonnieres.

There was something primal and special about that ritual. Even Xander seemed emotional as his mom finished and patted his chest. "The guests are still arriving, but we'll come get you when it's time," Mom said as she turned to go, and she dashed up the stairs before her emotions got the better of her.

We were collected by my sisters, who were dressed in opposite attire. Jenny was in a little tux—she refused to wear dresses these days—and Chelsie was in the frilliest thing I'd ever seen. We walked out of the house and into a frenzy of activity. It was a good thing I owned so much land because it was absolutely filled with people. Chairs were stretched from the river back to the house.

"Good thing we went with a microphone," I said under my breath.

We stood at the back of the crowd, and someone played the wedding march. I glanced at my parents, who stood at my arm, and then over to Ellen, who stood next to Xander. Lucy and the girls had agreed to follow behind with Brandon and Cliff, who were standing with us at the altar.

I took Xander's hand, and we marched up the aisle. With each step, I became more emotional. I hated that about myself. Since coming back to Wilcox, I seem to have become a total ninny. But when we finally arrived at the altar, I saw my sweet Xander also had tears.

We both chuckled at the mess on our faces, and I would've kissed him had Mayor Polly not asked who represented us today and a loud "we do" went up from all our family, including, if I wasn't wrong, my two sisters.

Of course that caused the entire crowd to laugh. "Well, that's certainly thorough," Polly said. She had been officially ordained as a minister so she would be able to officiate at our wedding. It was now a running joke that she wanted to be called Reverend Mayor instead of just Mayor.

We went through the wedding, my heart bursting at the seams. "Now, you boys have prepared vows?" Polly asked.

I nodded. "Xander, I was so surprised to fall in love with you. I didn't think it was possible to love someone so much and so intensely. You've brought so much light into my life, as well as a lot of work," I said, which got a chuckle from the crowd. "I gladly give myself to you in marriage, and I look forward to having you in my arms for the rest of my life."

Xander wiped at a tear and smiled. "Rhys, you have become the brightest star in the darkest night for me. You've added color to my life, and like you, I never knew how much I could love someone. You've sacrificed for our relationship and have fought for me to be the best I can be—not just in my work life but also in my emotional life. You have given me hope and direction. I hope to spend the rest of my life doing the same for you."

I took a deep breath and let it out slowly, absorbing all the love from Xander. His words struck my heart, and it was hard to express how much I felt for him.

"Do you have the rings?" Polly asked, and Lucy prompted the girls to get up and come forward.

Jenny handed Xander one ring, and Chelsie handed me the other. "Repeat after me," Polly said, and we went through the traditional ceremony of exchanging rings. Of course, the wedding rings snapped beautifully into the engagement rings, completing the symbolism that we were officially joined spiritually, emotionally, and legally.

"I now pronounce these two men husbands. You may now kiss, but keep it PG-rated," Polly declared.

I chuckled as Xander pulled me into a delicious, but definitely not PG-rated, kiss. The crowd's calls and whistles caused us to pull apart with matching smiles. "Hey, husband," Xander said.

"Hey back at you, husband," I replied.

"Come on, let's go eat cake."

That night was magical. We ate, danced, laughed with neighbors and friends, and had a beautiful party before we climbed into Xander's truck, loaded with blown-up condoms and every sort of ridiculousness the town's teenagers had decorated it with. I also suspected Brandon and Levi had a lot to do with the choices.

Right before we left, Mom shoved a bouquet in each of our hands and yelled that anyone single, no matter the sex, age, or willingness, had to step to the floor. They swirled us round and round, then faced us the opposite way to the single folks behind us. "Now, throw your bouquets," she demanded.

I threw mine backward while Xander stumbled a bit from being dizzy. His mom grabbed him and ended up with the bouquet in her hand. Of course, the shock on her face made me laugh out loud.

I turned to see who'd caught my bouquet and saw a very red-faced Jason staring back at me. "Looks like you caught it," I said, and Jason smiled sheepishly and shrugged. "Here, you take it," he said, trying to shove it into the hands of a very old widower standing next to him.

"Oh no, son, that curse is on you," the old man said, and the entire group laughed.

Xander leaned over and whispered in his mom's ear so only I could hear. "Looks like you might be stuck with that curse as well."

Ellen blanched and shook her head. "Nope, I've served my time," she yelled as she threw the bouquet into the crowd. Not one person touched it. They separated like the flowers were filled with broken glass. Of course, that just got another rise out of everyone.

Jason picked up the flowers and walked them back to Mom. "Come on. We'll grab a few glasses of champagne and mourn our fates together."

Xander and I spent the night in Portland and then flew to Hawaii, where we intended to waste a perfectly beautiful island by making love over and over and over in our room.

I hadn't understood weddings until my own. I thought they were mostly bullshit, but damn, there was no one I'd rather be with than Xander Petterson. The wedding and celebration made sense now. As did the honeymoon. I wanted everything Xander had or was willing to give me. What a great way to celebrate our new lives together.

Xander

RHYS'S DAD and Lucy moved into their new home while we were on our honeymoon. Thank goodness, because that left Xander and me alone in our home. I didn't mean to brag, but during the honeymoon, I'd learned a trick or two about making Rhys get loud during sex. I wanted to work on perfecting those new skills.

We'd just fallen asleep on the couch in each other's arms, both of us a little jet-lagged from the trip back from Hawaii. The television was still on, but the news was more soothing than distracting.

My mind drifted in the way it does when you're dreaming. I saw the old house where Aunt Greta lived when I was little. Except it wasn't dilapidated. It looked new in my dream. At first I stood alone, staring at the house, but suddenly Rhys was there with me.

I looked down and smiled at him, thinking, even in my dream, how lucky I was to be married to that incredible man.

When I looked up, Aunt Greta and Rhys's Aunt Helen were sitting on the front porch swing. They waved at us, and then Helen said, "We're so proud of you boys. You've found love in life in a way we never could."

Aunt Greta looked at Aunt Helen, love firmly in her expression. "We've found it now, though, my dearest. That's what matters."

"Love," Aunt Greta said, looking back at us. "That's what matters."

I startled awake and looked over at Rhys, who was sitting up. "I just had the most bizarre dream," he said.

I laughed. "Um, old house, Aunt Greta and your aunt Helen on a front porch swing?"

Rhys paled but nodded.

I leaned over and kissed him. "Roll with it. I'm guessing that was their way of saying they're at peace."

He nodded, leaned back into me, and said, "Love is what matters, right?"

Keep Reading for an Excerpt from
Bridging Lives
By Greyson McCoy!

Cliff

"I'M NOT evacuating, Walt," I shouted, refusing to look my elderly neighbor in the face. "I just got these plants in the ground, and I'm not going to let a stupid wildfire destroy them all."

"Cliff," he said pointedly, "your father wouldn't have stayed."

His mention of my dad brought me up short, but I didn't have time for this. Not when everything my family had worked for was at stake.

"Walt, if I leave, if I miss watering for even a day, the crop will die," I said, not hiding my exasperation. "Two hundred tomato plants, three hundred seventy-five squash and zucchini plants. Not to mention the corn, the beans, the—"

Walt put his hand up. "Son, I know. I totally understand, but your life is worth more. Think about what your parents would've done."

I shook my head in desperation. I'd have to go eventually, but I was conflicted about abandoning my farm. "If the fire reaches Mayfield, I'll evacuate."

"You're a man of your word, so that's good enough for me," Walt said. He turned to go, then quickly disappeared into the smoke.

Spring in this part of California was usually wet, but not this year. The drought had stretched through the winter, and now a heat wave baked us drier than a popcorn fart, as my dad used to say.

I pulled on his old respirator mask as I entered the greenhouse, because the smoke was even more concentrated inside. Typically, I didn't plant anything until May, but the warm winter and spring had prompted me to get a head start.

That was good because it opened up the greenhouse for herbs. In recent years we'd made almost as much on those as the other crops. With the crops in the field, I now had all my tender herb plants growing in here.

I glanced around at the plants I'd spent the past several months cultivating. Even if the fire destroyed the fields, if I could save these plants, I'd still have a farm and enough income to at least pay the taxes on the place. My crops might burn, but I'd be damned if I let my family's legacy go up in smoke too.

The old refrigerated truck Dad had used to transport produce to the farmers' markets sat beside the house. I rushed over and hurriedly slid the plant shelves inside it.

"You need to go." I could hear my father's voice in my head, but his authoritative tone didn't slow me down. Both my parents died a year ago, but I still sometimes heard them. Most days, I found their presence more comforting than concerning. It helped me pretend that they were still around. I had even taken to responding to them out loud, but only when alone, lest anyone think I'd gone off my rocker.

"Dad, I can't lose these plants. You know what that'd mean for the farm."

There was no response, but I could feel him. He wasn't happy with me staying.

"All I need is an hour to pack the truck," I said, as if negotiating with my father's ghost would keep the fire at bay.

I pulled my phone out of my pocket and clicked on the local news app while I made a quick dash inside the house. The forecaster reported the rapidly spreading wildfire was thirty miles outside Mayfield and the wind had picked up. The worst was going to happen. I could feel it deep in my bones.

Mom had long ago developed an evacuation plan, and when fire broke out within a hundred-mile radius of our farm, she began to pack. She'd ingrained disaster preparedness in me over the years, and it had practically become family tradition. Most everything my mom considered valuable was packed in a chest near the front door during the last evacuation and still sat there.

I raced to my bedroom to pack some clothes and other incidentals, like my phone charger, that I might need. This wasn't my first fire-fleeing rodeo. We'd fled from wildfire several times over the years, but this one was hitting different. For the first time, I had all my parents' belongings to consider.

I hadn't entered their bedroom since the accident. It had been frozen in time since that awful day. It hurt too much to see their things. They'd driven to the city for a party and were simply in the wrong place at the wrong time. A drunk driver had gone down a ramp the wrong way and hit them head-on at over seventy miles per hour. "It was fast. They didn't even know what hit them," a police officer told me. That was good, I guessed. I took some comfort in knowing they hadn't suffered, though the pain I felt at losing them would never go away.

I ignored the knot in my stomach as I rifled through their things. I found the only tie Dad ever wore. It was ugly as homemade sin, but I gave it to him when I was five or six, and he'd worn it as proudly as if it were a designer brand.

Next, I found Mom's scarf, the only thing she ever knitted. The stitching was off, and I remember her mumbling curses to herself while she struggled through it. It was so unlike her, but that's why I cherished the memory. Dad's ugly tie and Mom's pitiful scarf—the two things that would always make me think of them.

Mom's jewelry was already packed in the evacuation chest, although she had never worn any of it. "Farmers don't have much use for jewelry," she said in my mind. Still, some of it had been passed down from her mother, so it had sentimental value.

Mom had also packed away some memorabilia, including my college diploma. She was ridiculously proud when I was accepted to university and prouder still when I graduated. "My baby is the first of the Baker crew to earn a college degree," she said, beaming. Baker was Mom's maiden name. I never brought up that my cousin Levi was a year older and got his degree before I did.

Dad's brother had college degrees, not that he needed them. My uncle was wealthy and snooty—not worth looking up to, not worth my time. He hadn't even come to my parents' funeral. His absence was confirmation enough that we might be related but he wasn't family.

I pulled my respirator mask back on as I rushed outside with my irreplaceable family treasures and tossed them all into the old trailer that I could pull behind the refrigerator truck.

By the time I finished hitching them together, the news app was reporting that the fire had reached Mayfield. Despite my promise to Walt to clear out once it hit town, I couldn't leave yet. I still needed to rescue the plants, and I didn't have much time left. I drove the truck out to the greenhouse and began loading plants onto trays. Even in my hurry, I had to be careful and methodical. If I damaged the plants or they slid around in the truck, they'd be no good to me in the end.

I'd been at it for a while when Walt pulled his ancient pickup in front of mine. The minute he got out, he yelled, "You need to get out of here, time's up. The fire's ripping through town."

A sense of dread suddenly came over me. It was as if I could feel my dad pushing me to leave.

I shoved my respirator mask off. "I just need thirty more minutes."

"You don't have thirty minutes," Walt said. Walt grabbed a half-filled tray and slid it onto a shelf in the truck before I could load what was left.

"You're as stubborn as your daddy ever was," Walt said.

"Where's Martha?" I asked, and he said his better half had already evacuated.

"I knew you'd still be out here acting like a fool. I'm not willing to let you die for some plants, boy," he yelled. "I'll drag you out of here kicking and screaming if I have to. Don't think I won't."

Hearing the old man's voice break snapped me out of my tunnel vision. The smoke had grown thick, and I could feel the increased heat around us. The fire was close. I was leaving good plants behind, but I closed the greenhouse door on them, climbed into the truck, and followed Walt off the farm and onto Bigford Road. We'd only gone a few miles when I saw the red glow. Until that moment, I hadn't really believed the wildfire would destroy my family's farm, Walt's farm, and all the homes in the area. Now it seemed more like a certainty.

Tears flowed when I drove past Rhonda Greene's farm, already ablaze. I wiped them away as we then went through an area burning on both sides of the road. At least the road remained passable. I had to focus on that, on the literal road ahead, rather than the destruction all around us.

Thirty minutes later we pulled into the Chevron station in Weaverville and filled up with gas. "The evacuation center is at the school," Walt told me. "Martha called and said it's a crowded mess, but our neighbors are all there and safe."

"I can't keep the plants in the truck for long, and they won't have anywhere to store them at the center. What should I do?" I asked Walt.

"I don't know, son. All the surrounding counties are under states of emergency too."

Adrenaline was still pumping through me, so I hadn't thought about the full ramifications of what all this meant until that moment. But seeing the weariness on Walt's face, it hit me hard. "It's gone, isn't it?" I said. "The whole town, all our farms, everything."

He glanced away, and I knew his emotions were getting the better of him. He took a moment to get himself under control and then said, "Let's go on over to the evacuation center and let everyone know we made it out okay. We'll figure the rest out then."

I found a shady space to park on the outskirts of the center's nearly full parking lot. The truck's refrigeration only worked sporadically and almost always broke down when the truck was parked. The temperature was already too hot for the plants, and if experience proved true, it would only get worse by noon.

I followed Walt inside and was overwhelmed by the number of people I recognized from the community. Since I knew most of them, I figured the faces I didn't recognize must've been people from the surrounding areas. A desk was set up with a volunteer who wrote down my name and phone number.

After we located Martha, who greeted us with hugs and a relieved smile, I found a quiet corner of the gym and called my aunt and uncle. Between the local news coverage and the chatter circulating in the center, I knew the wildfire had become national news.

My mom's sister answered on the first ring. "Hello, Cliff?" she asked, sounding stressed.

"Hi, Aunt Sue. I wanted to let y'all know I'm safe. I made it out, and I'm at the evacuation center in Weaverville."

"Oh, thank the Lord. We were so worried."

My uncle interrupted her. "Does it look like the fire is headed toward the farm?" he asked.

It took me a moment to get my emotions under control enough to answer. "It was headed that way when I left. The farm is probably gone."

I didn't know for sure, and wouldn't be a hundred percent convinced until I could lay my own eyes on the land, but I could feel it. The home where I'd grown up, the greenhouse Dad and I had built together, the fertile fields we'd spent years cultivating—all destroyed by nature. It was almost like I'd been connected to the farm on a soul level and felt the life drain out of it.

"Come here, Cliff, to Wilcox," my aunt said. "We've got the space now Levi has moved out. You can have his old room."

"I don't know, Aunt Sue. I'm still trying to figure things out."

Aunt Sue had struggled when I came out as gay a few years back. She'd told me she loved me, but I could still feel a subtle strain in our relationship. That could've been me projecting my own fear of rejection, but I still wasn't entirely sure where things stood with her.

My cousin Levi, on the other hand, had been cool about it, even saying he had a friend he could fix me up with. When I acted interested, he laughed his butt off. He'd married his high school sweetheart, Keya, last year and moved down the road from his parents. Levi had grown up on his parents' large traditional dairy farm and still helped his dad with some of the day-to-day operations.

"Uncle Chris, is that okay with you? If I come to Oregon?"

"Of course," he said, sounding surprised. "Why would you even ask?"

I didn't have the nerve to admit it was because I was afraid he wouldn't be okay with me being gay. Aunt Sue and Levi were the only two I'd discussed that with. Uncle Chris wasn't there when we talked, and although I figured Aunt Sue had informed him at some point, I didn't know how he felt about it.

"I am what I am, Uncle Chris."

"What you are is family, and we want you to come here," he said without hesitation.

Tears ran down my face. "I'm gonna talk to some people here. Then I'll let you know what my plans are. Thank you for being there for me."

When we hung up, I had to take a moment to get myself together.

Walt found me with my forehead resting against the wall, and he placed a hand on my shoulder. "They're setting up cots and bringing in food and supplies," he said as he gave my shoulder a comforting squeeze. "They said we could stay here as long as we need."

"I think I'm gonna head to Oregon to be with my mom's sister and her family. They just invited me to stay with them."

"That's probably best. It'll be a while before they let us get back out there anyway."

"Will you let me know when they do?" I asked, embarrassed by my childlike tone. I sounded small, even to my own ears, but couldn't help it. I felt utterly defeated.

"Of course. You gonna wait till tomorrow to leave?"

"No, I'm worried about the seedlings. I won't have time to restart them, and if I can salvage any harvest this year—"

"I know, son, I know," Walt said, patting my back.

"Okay, I'm gonna head out as soon as possible. My uncle has a greenhouse. Hopefully I can use it to store the plants until I figure out the next steps."

Walt nodded and accompanied me back to the check-in desk. I let the volunteer know I'd be in Oregon and Walt and Martha would handle any immediate issues regarding my land.

I had to fill out paperwork, and the sheriff wanted to see me before I left, so I couldn't get away until much later than I wanted.

I gave Walt and Martha hugs goodbye. Then I finally climbed into the truck and called my aunt and uncle to tell them I was on my way. "I need your greenhouse, if it's available. I'm bringing several hundred plants with me that I saved."

"That'll be fine," Uncle Chris said. "We'll empty the shelves so it'll be ready when you arrive."

When I hung up, I gave in to my emotions and let myself weep. I couldn't fully digest that my family's farm was gone. I had the insurance papers in the trailer, thanks to Mom's previous evacuation packing, but I hadn't looked at the policy's value. It had cost an arm and a leg to keep the insurance paid, so I assumed it had to be significant, but I doubted I'd ever rebuild unless it was in the millions. Money had always been tight, but I had never known any different. My parents had chosen farming, and I couldn't imagine my life without it.

Despite inheriting the land from them, most of Dad's family were city dwellers from San Francisco. They hated everything about our lifestyle and ostracized us for it. But Mom and her sister had come from farm life and embraced it for their own families. That's why I was bound for tiny Wilcox, Oregon. Farming was all I knew, and a truckload of plants was all I had left of it.

I PULLED INTO my aunt and uncle's around eleven that evening. Despite the fatigue, I smiled when I saw the sign for Owens Century Farm that stood high over their driveway. I'd driven straight through without stopping for anything other than gas and restroom visits. I had never been one to eat when stressed, even though I could still hear one of my mom's recurring lectures regarding how important it was to keep my strength up. But I'd been too focused on getting to Oregon and hopefully saving the seedlings to worry about food.

Uncle Chris had to get up before dawn to milk the cows, so I wasn't surprised the lights were out in the house. Instead of waking them up, I lay across the bench seat in my truck and let myself fall asleep. I was startled awake by a knock on the driver's side window.

"Cliff, honey, get up and come on in for some breakfast."

I sat up and rubbed the sleep from my eyes. My aunt Sue was the spitting image of my mom, and in the morning sunlight, it took me a moment to realize who it was. I blinked back the tears and shook my head to get rid of the cobwebs.

My stomach rumbled loudly when I entered the house and smelled bacon and eggs. Aunt Sue pulled me into a hug before I could sit down at the table. "I'm glad you came, Cliff. I was so worried." She turned quickly and rushed to dish me up a plate. I didn't let myself ponder the sadness in her voice. I couldn't let myself get into that kind of emotional state, not right now anyway.

I sat beside Uncle Chris at the table, and he put his hand on my shoulder and squeezed it tight. The gesture was his way of letting me know I was welcome.

When Aunt Sue reappeared, she placed a mound of steaming hot food in front of me. "You want coffee?" she asked.

"Yes, please, ma'am."

She returned a moment later with a half-empty pot. I must've looked confused since neither she nor Uncle Chris drank coffee. Aunt Sue smiled. "Levi's been here," she said, and I had to laugh.

I dug into the homemade biscuits and gravy and the bacon and fresh eggs. My mother was attacked by a rooster when she was little, so she was afraid of chickens, and we'd never raised any. But the rest of the spread mirrored the huge breakfasts Mom used to make, and her sister's cooking tasted just as delicious.

Aunt Sue and Uncle Chris were strangely quiet as we ate. "Everything okay?" I asked.

"Are *you* okay?" Uncle Chris asked. "You've been through a lot in the past day."

I shook my head. I didn't feel okay, but I also didn't feel like breaking down again. I had my hands full with saving the plants, operating on minimal sleep, and combating the stress of losing my parents and our family farm in the span of a year.

Fortunately they didn't push. When I took my dishes to the sink, my aunt shooed me out of the kitchen. "You go with Chris. Those seedlings won't live long in the back of that truck," she said.

Uncle Chris was a stoic man. Salt of the earth, as my dad always said. That was what I needed right now—someone who could help me get the work done first and worry about emotions later.

The greenhouse sat next to a large historic dairy barn. Chris's grandparents built the barn when they started the dairy, but Uncle Chris installed a more modern system when he took over operations. The old barn now housed equipment instead of animals, and the old milking shed had been converted into a greenhouse so they could extend their growing season. But it'd been vacant for as long as I could remember.

I unhooked the trailer where Uncle Chris said it would be safe and out of the way. Then I pulled the old truck around to the greenhouse, inspected the space, and began to unload the trays.

Luckily, most of the plants had made the trip safely. One tray, the partial one I'd run out of time filling, had a few damaged plants, but it looked like I'd be able to save most of them. Uncle Chris connected a hose while I finished unloading. I watered the plants immediately and hoped it wouldn't be too much of a shock.

I knew it was ridiculous that I wanted to save the plants, but it felt important. My gut told me I wouldn't be returning to my farm this year, if ever. Those plants were the only *living* thing I had left of my life in California, and I couldn't just let that go.

With the plants tended to, Uncle Chris headed out to do some farm chores. He waved me off when I offered to help. "Today is for rest, but I'll gladly put you to work tomorrow. Just remember, the girls don't tolerate tardiness," he said. He'd made that same joke about his cows before, and I found his humor comforting.

Confident my seedlings would be okay, I drove back to the house and parked the truck next to the trailer.

Then I gave Walt a call.

"Hello?" he answered.

"Hi, Walt. I'm in Oregon. How are you and Martha? Have you heard any updates?"

"We're okay, son. Still holed up in the evacuation center. Word is the fire continues to rage, and they haven't told us which properties, if any, made it through. It's all still just wait and see."

"I figured that'd be the case. Just wanted to check in on you both."

"That's mighty appreciated. This won't come as a surprise, but my Martha has taken it upon herself to ensure everyone in this place gets fed on the regular. Truth be told, I think her keeping busy helps keep her mind off everything else. Anyway, how was the drive to your aunt's place?" he asked.

"Thankfully uneventful. I drove straight through, so I'm gonna go crash now."

"The plants?" he asked.

"Nearly every single one made it. My uncle helped me get them into his greenhouse. They're watered and looking fine."

"Good, son. I'm really glad."

I sighed. "Thanks, Walt. I don't think I'd have gotten out in time if it weren't for you."

"That's what neighbors are for," he said, and I had to hold my breath to keep from completely losing it. That's not the way everyone's neighbors were. Just the ones I'd grown up with, the ones whose homes had likely burned to the ground along with mine. My parents and I regarded them as lifelong friends.

"Okay, well, let me know if you hear anything," I said.

When I returned to the house, my aunt took one look at me and sent me to Levi's old room. I loved that she didn't dote on me, since I didn't have the emotional capacity to deal with it. What I needed was matter-of-fact support and more sleep, and luckily it appeared that's exactly what I would get.

SCAN THE QR CODE
BELOW TO ORDER!

GREYSON McCOY loves to travel. After years of being tied down to a life of kids, work, running a small farm, and all things domestic, he and his husband have taken full advantage of their empty nest to travel the world.

The joy of writing came to Greyson late in life. While completing his master's degree, he found himself fighting between desperately wanting to write fiction and finishing the homework and papers he'd been assigned.

After his master's was finished, Greyson decided to shirk his life of responsibility and pursue his dream of writing full time. His stories reflect many of the locations he and his husband have visited over the years.

Visit Greyson McCoy on his website at www.GreysonMcCoy.gay (his husband assures him that's a real domain extension) and sign up for his newsletter to stay informed of his journey in the world of romance and all things love.

Follow me on BookBub

BRIDGING HEARTS ▪ BOOK ONE

Bridging Hope

Raising kids
and finding
love is
impossible,
isn't it?

GREYSON McCOY

When workaholic Pierce Simms's sister passes, he suddenly finds himself unemployed, back in the hometown he fled, and raising his niece and nephew. Despite that, he's confident he has things under control—at least until his sister's high-school sweetheart shows up.

With his teaching grant ended, Dalton O'Dell is at loose ends and tight purse strings. Just as the world crashes down on him, he learns his ex-girlfriend has passed and named him guardian of her two young children. Chaos ensues when he and her brother, Pierce, are forced together to raise the toddlers in Pierce's family farmhouse.

Nestled in the enchanting beauty of the farm, Pierce and Dalton bond over the challenges of co-parenting and their shared grief as unexpected love blossoms. Love might not be enough, however, if they can't learn to bridge the gap between their different worlds and overcome the trauma of their pasts.

SCAN THE QR CODE BELOW TO ORDER!

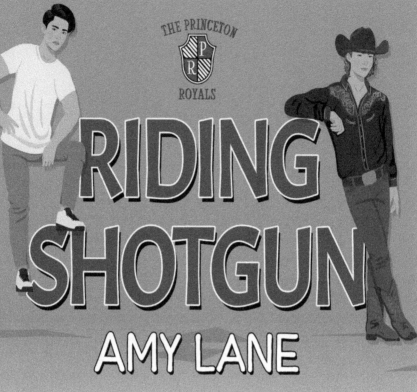

THE PRINCETON ROYALS

RIDING SHOTGUN

AMY LANE

Leaving California

THE PRINCETON ROYALS

TEXAS
THIS WAY

THEIR BLOODLINE MAY NOT BE ROYAL,
BUT THE FAMILY ATTITUDE CERTAINLY IS.

Val Royal's tight family has always had his back, but they love to interfere in his life. That interference almost sends him over the edge when they arrange for Rory McCauley, security specialist, marksman, and hound-dog smartass, to ride shotgun as security on his latest run.

Hot, bossy, and sharp as a tack, Val ticks all Rory's boxes, but Val's looking for something real, and Rory's allergic to intimacy. Besides, their gig running refrigerated bull semen from Bakersfield to Austin could make or break Val's buddy's ranch, so Val's understandably pretty focused on the job. Rory still wishes Val would let him help Val, uh, ***relax.***

As Val and Rory work to keep their payload safe from a couple of determined saboteurs and they get to know each other as smart, competent, fearless professionals, sparks fly, and Val starts to fall for Rory's roguish charm. But can he convince Rory their romance would be worth more than a straight shot to Austin—that it would be a love worth coming home to?

SCAN THE QR CODE
BELOW TO ORDER!

How can they be together when
they live in different worlds?

The Duke's Cowboy

COWBOY NOBILITY ♥ BOOK ONE

ANDREW GREY

Cowboy Nobility: Book One

George Lester, the Duke of Northumberland, flees familial expectations in Britain for the promise of freedom of San Francisco, looking for the chance to be himself. But before he even gets close, a blizzard forces him off the road, and he finds himself freezing half to death in a small town with no motel… with a litter of puppies to look after.

Luckily for George, he also finds Alan.

As the heir to his family's ranch, Alan Justice knows the burden of being the oldest son. He doesn't have time to show George, the stranger his brother dragged home, what it takes to be a cowboy. But that very night, George surprises him by helping a mare in distress through a difficult birth. Maybe the duke is made of sterner stuff than Alan thought.

George and Alan keep surprising each other, and every day they grow a little closer. But when George's responsibilities call him home, Alan finds he's the one who has something to prove—that he can handle what it means to be the duke's cowboy.

Scan the QR Code
Below to Order!

Two weeks together
will have to be
enough....

The
Viscount's
Rancher

COWBOY NOBILITY ♥ BOOK TWO

ANDREW GREY

Cowboy Nobility: Book Two

Viscount Collin Northington has spent his life under his father's thumb. When his friend George and his cowboy husband, Alan, offer to let him tag along to the US for two weeks, Collin jumps at the chance to get away. Perhaps the open ranges of Wyoming will put his problems into perspective. He even dreams of meeting a cowboy of his own.

He doesn't expect his dreams to come true.

When Tank Rogers returned home after his military service, he took over the family ranch the way he knew he was meant to. Now he's the only one left, but he likes the solitude. Even so, he has no excuse to object to putting up Alan's friend for a few weeks in exchange for some help around the ranch—it wouldn't be neighborly.

The feelings he has for his blue-blooded houseguest aren't exactly neighborly either.

Once Tank realizes there's more to Collin than upper-crust manners, suddenly his solitary life holds a lot less appeal. But in the long term, Tank doesn't fit into Collin's fancy society life any more than Collin fits into Tank's down-home and dusty ranch... does he?

SCAN THE QR CODE
BELOW TO ORDER!

THE TASTE OF
DESERT
GREEN

Is their love an oasis,
or only a mirage?

KIM FIELDING

Struggling business owner George is stuck in the past. Rootless Zephyr lives only in the present. Can they find the courage to build a future together?

At thirty years old, George Harlow is at risk of becoming as fossilized as the prehistoric tourist attraction he inherited—the one that's headed the way of the dinosaurs. Even if staying afloat didn't take all his energy, the dating pool in his town is as dry as the desert surrounding it. As for the family trauma from his past? That can stay buried.

Then Zephyr Steiber blows into his life.

Zephyr lives up to his name, drifting wherever Fate takes him, sometimes renting his body in exchange for a ride. With his high heels and lace and bright personality, Zephyr brings a spark of life to George's dried-up existence.

For a while Zephyr is content to shelter in George's refuge and to be George's solace in return. Together they create an oasis. But with Zephyr haunted by the ghosts of bad decisions, and with George's home and livelihood threatened by a global pandemic, can their tentative dreams for a future together survive reality?

SCAN THE QR CODE
BELOW TO ORDER!